Don't miss out on any of our books in March!

This month, Lynne Graham brings you *The Italian Billionaire's Pregnant Bride*, the last story in her brilliant trilogy THE RICH, THE RUTHLESS AND THE REALLY HANDSOME, where tycoon Sergio Torrente demands that pregnant Kathy marry him. In *The Spaniard's Pregnancy Proposal* by Kim Lawrence, Antonio Rochas is sexy, smoldering and won't let relationship-shy Fleur go easily! In Trish Morey's *The Sheikh's Convenient Virgin*, a devastatingly handsome desert prince is in need of a convenient wife who must be pure. Anne Mather brings you a brooding Italian who believes Juliet is a gold-digger in *Bedded for the Italian's Pleasure*. In *Taken by Her Greek Boss* by Cathy Williams, Nick Papaeliou can't understand why he's attracted to frumpy Rose—but her shapeless garments hide a very alluring woman. Lindsay Armstrong's *From Waif to His Wife* tells the story of a rich businessman who avoids marriage— but one woman's sensual spell clouds his perfect judgment! In *The Millionaire's Convenient Bride* by Catherine George, a dashing millionaire needs a temporary housekeeper—but soon the business arrangement includes a wedding! Finally, in *One-Night Love Child* by Anne McAllister, Flynn doesn't know he's the father of Sara's son—but when he discovers the truth he *will* possess her.... Happy reading from Harlequin Presents!

EXPECTING!

She's sexy,
successful…
and
PREGNANT!

Relax and enjoy our fabulous series about
couples whose passion ends in pregnancies…
sometimes unexpected!

Share the surprises, emotions, drama and
suspense as our parents-to-be come to terms
with the prospect of bringing a new baby
into the world. All will discover that the
business of making babies brings with it
the most special love of all….

Delivered only by Harlequin Presents®

Kim Lawrence

THE SPANIARD'S PREGNANCY PROPOSAL

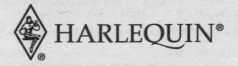

TORONTO • NEW YORK • LONDON
AMSTERDAM • PARIS • SYDNEY • HAMBURG
STOCKHOLM • ATHENS • TOKYO • MILAN • MADRID
PRAGUE • WARSAW • BUDAPEST • AUCKLAND

ISBN-13: 978-0-373-12708-5
ISBN-10:   0-373-12708-1

THE SPANIARD'S PREGNANCY PROPOSAL

First North American Publication 2008.

Copyright © 2006 by Kim Lawrence.

This is a work of fiction. Names, characters, places and incidents are either the product of the author's imagination or are used fictitiously, and any resemblance to actual persons, living or dead, business establishments, events or locales is entirely coincidental.

This edition published by arrangement with Harlequin Books S.A.

® and TM are trademarks of the publisher. Trademarks indicated with ® are registered in the United States Patent and Trademark Office, the Canadian Trade Marks Office and in other countries.

www.eHarlequin.com

Printed in U.S.A.

All about the author...
Kim Lawrence

Though lacking much authentic Welsh blood,
KIM LAWRENCE—from English/Irish stock—was
born and brought up in north Wales. She returned
there when she married, and her sons were both
born on Anglesey, an island off the coast. Though
not isolated, Anglesey is a little off the beaten
track, but lively Dublin, which Kim loves, is only a
short ferry ride away.

Today they live on the farm her husband was
brought up on. Welsh is the first language of many
people in this area, and Kim's husband and sons
are all bilingual. She is having a lot of fun, not
to mention a few headaches, trying to learn the
language!

With small children, she thought the unsocial
hours of nursing weren't too attractive, so,
encouraged by a husband who thinks she can
do anything she sets her mind to, Kim tried her
hand at writing. Always a keen Harlequin reader, it
seemed natural for her to write a romance novel.
Now she can't imagine doing anything else.

She is a keen gardener and cook, and enjoys
running—often on the beach because, since she
lives on an island, the sea is never very far away.
She is usually accompanied by her Jack Russell,
Sprout—don't ask, it's a long story!

CHAPTER ONE

FLEUR STEWART woke up and after a few minutes of lying there listening to bird song she forced her eyelids open. Yawning, she squinted at the clock on the bedside table. It was eight-thirty.

It was also her birthday. She was twenty-five, an entire quarter of a century. She resisted the temptation to ask herself what she had done with the first twenty-five years, because that would have inevitably led to her asking herself what she planned to do with the next twenty-five.

And Fleur didn't know.

She wasn't making any plans at all. She was going with the flow. Because life, she reflected, pulling the duvet over her head and burrowing down, never quite turned out the way you expected.

She had only ever wanted to act. The dream had been born the day her parents had taken her to see a matinee performance of a West End musical when she was eight. It had died midway through her second term at drama school. To be precise, on the day she had badly botched an audition everyone had thought was hers and realised that the only thing standing between her and a glittering career was a complete absence of talent.

The next day, and still in the same self-pitying, despond-ent frame of mind, she had met Adam Moore, a final-year law student. Good-looking Adam had been incredibly supportive and sympathetic when, over her second glass of wine, she had confided her doubts. A kindred spirit, he had seen her point immediately. What was the point staying on at drama school if you were only ever going to be mediocre?

This had been a lot easier to hear than, 'You've got to develop a thicker skin,' which was the attitude her friends, who hadn't taken her crisis of confidence seriously, had adopted.

Adam had told her that a girl with her brains could do a lot better for herself than acting and Fleur had been flattered and believed him. Or at least she had convinced herself she believed him. Deep down even then Fleur had known that what she was really doing was choosing the easy option.

Three months later she and Adam had been engaged and she'd been happily waiting tables. And if she'd ever stopped to wonder what she was doing or ask herself if she was *really* happy, she'd reminded herself that this was a purely tempo-rary measure. And the tips had been very good, which had been great because it had made sense for Adam to concen-trate on his studies without worrying about little things like paying the rent.

Contemplating the painful naïveté of her younger self in-evitably made Fleur despise herself, so she tried hard not to revisit the past. She tried to live in the present.

The present was actually surprisingly good.

Four years on there was no Adam. Admittedly there was no stage career either, but happily she was no longer waiting tables!

She loved her job teaching drama at the local college. Her colleagues were a decent bunch, the work was challenging and she loved the buzz of being around young, and, for the most part, enthusiastic people. If ever any of her students felt like throwing in the towel, Fleur told them that, sure, they might not have what it took, but they'd never know for sure if they didn't show a little backbone when the going got tough.

The biggest plus of the job was that nobody here knew about her recent history. That being so, there were none of the sympathetic looks she hated or 'I do admire you, you're so brave for getting on with your life'—as if she had a choice—remarks to deal with.

No matter how much you enjoyed your job it was still a nice feeling come Saturday to wake up and pull the covers over your head and have a nice lazy lie-in. This Saturday, birthday or no, the lie-in was not a long one. The late-August sun shining through the thin curtains of her bedroom was just too tempting. It made her think of blackberries, walking the rescue dog her friend Jane had foisted on her the previous month and the million and one things that needed doing in the garden.

For a town girl she had adapted to the rural existence really well.

Fleur was still in her pyjamas when the phone rang.

She set aside an unopened birthday card and took a slurp of her freshly brewed coffee before padding barefoot through to the hallway to answer it.

'Happy Birthday!' The sound of Jane's voice brought a smile to her face. Jane, a fashion photographer with copper hair and a sarcastic tongue, was the sort of person whose enthusiasm for life was infectious.

Sometimes Fleur wished she had half of Jane's energy. It was Jane who had encouraged her to move out of London after the miscarriage, and after Adam's infidelity had been exposed, and it had been Jane who had told her to go for it when the job in the drama department had been advertised.

'Did you get my card?'

'I was just about to open it.'

'I wish I could be there. Next week, though, we'll really let down our hair,' Jane promised. 'Get out your sexiest shoes, I have plans.'

Fleur winced. She had a horrible suspicion that her friend's plans would involve pushing her at a member of the opposite sex. The problem with Jane, she brooded, was she *imagined* she was subtle. She was anything but! 'There's not a lot of call for sexy shoes around here.'

'Now you just sound sad,' Jane informed her tartly. 'There is always room in a girl's life for sexy shoes. It makes me really mad when I think how you waste your legs.' She sighed enviously. 'Look at me—legs like a Welsh Corgi, but do I sit at home nights moping? No, I—'

'All right, I get the message,' Fleur protested. 'I'll make an effort.'

'Have you got anything planned for tonight?'

Fleur knew that admitting the only thing she had planned was a night in front of the TV would earn her a stern lecture on the need to *get out there,* so she got creative. 'A drink with some friends from work.' Nobody at work, where she had cultivated a reputation for being reserved, actually knew it was her birthday.

'Well, that's good. And how is our dog?'

'*Our* dog is eating his way through my furniture. I don't possess a chair without teeth marks. You've no idea how happy I am you decided I needed the company.'

An overlong pause followed her teasing comment.

'You know I'm only kidding…?' Fleur frowned. It wasn't like Jane not to come back with a sarcastic retort. 'I love the mutt.'

'It's not like you're not totally over him. You are, aren't you? Over him, that is.'

'I assume you're talking about Adam?' This much Fleur had managed to extract from her friend's disjointed monologue. 'I'm insulted you can ask, but, yes, I am very much over him.'

'Paula's pregnant,' Jane blurted. 'She and Adam are having a baby.'

It was a guilty-sounding Jane who eventually broke the lengthening silence.

'I'm sorry, Fleur, I didn't know whether to tell you…'

Fleur took a deep breath and pressed a hand to her churning stomach. *A baby…!*

She inhaled deeply, recognising her reaction to the news her ex-fiancé and his new wife were having a baby as irrational. Recognition didn't make the feeling go away; crazily it felt more of a betrayal than learning about his affair had.

'No, I'm glad you did, Jane,' she said, trying hard to sound as though she meant it.

'I thought Adam might have mentioned it…?'

'I haven't spoken to him for months.' Not since her ex-fiancé had married the woman she now knew he had started sleeping with while she'd been pregnant.

A perfectly natural reaction, he had belligerently claimed for a man who had found himself forced against his will into fatherhood. The implication, false though it was, that she had deliberately trapped him with the pregnancy had hurt and angered Fleur incredibly deeply at the time. But then she had still harboured some daft idea that her ex wasn't a total loser!

God, how was I ever that stupid?

'The slimy rat!' Jane, never one to hold back, observed viciously. 'That pair deserve one another.'

'I suppose Adam's allowed a life.'

With a sigh she brushed her hair from her face anchoring it at the nape of her neck, and wondered, Am I jealous? Not of Adam and Paula. She had long ago recognised that her feelings for Adam had never amounted to love, not the lasting variety. But maybe of what they had…?

What she would never have. It wasn't men she didn't trust, just her own judgement.

'After what he did to you! The only life *slimy rat* is allowed is one filled with misery and suffering!' Jane, not a big believer in turning the other cheek, bellowed down the other end of the line.

Holding the receiver away from her ear, Fleur heard Jane add bitterly, 'The man was in bed, *your bed,* with that woman when you were in hospital…sorry, Fleur,' she added immediately, sounding contrite. 'Me and my big mouth…I didn't mean to open old wounds.'

Fleur eased her bottom onto the edge of the small console table and fiddled with the top button of her pyjama jacket. 'Don't worry about it, Jane. I was going to find out some time,' she said, thinking some wounds never did heal. And the wound in question wasn't actually such an old one.

Sometimes it felt like a lifetime ago and other times it felt like yesterday, but in reality it had been eighteen months since Fleur had been rushed into Casualty midway through what had been a difficult pregnancy.

Jane, who had been there with her, had desperately tried to contact Adam for her while the grave-faced doctor had told Fleur that he was very sorry but there was no heartbeat.

'I do worry. It's my fault you split up…'

'Because you caught them in bed?' When she had not been able to locate Adam Jane had offered to go to the flat to fetch Fleur's night things. She had found more than she had expected! 'Don't be stupid, Jane. How could it possibly be your fault?' Fleur protested angrily.

'They say personal tragedy can make people closer than

ever…?' From her voice Fleur could imagine the look of guilt on Jane's face. 'If I'd just—'

Fleur cut her off. 'If we'd been that close I doubt if you'd have found him in bed with someone else.'

In retrospect it didn't seem possible that she had missed the signs that Adam was having an affair. Nothing had clicked with her—not his unexplained absences, or the caller who had always rung off when Fleur had picked up the phone. Fleur had been concerned, but only about Adam's increasing resentment of the restrictions the doctors had placed on her after the threatened miscarriage earlier on in her pregnancy.

'He started an affair with Paula weeks after we moved into the flat.' And it is *not* my fault, she told herself firmly. 'You and I both know that the split-up was inevitable. If I hadn't fallen pregnant I think it would have happened sooner,' she admitted.

Once she had discovered she was having a baby, Fleur had pushed her growing doubts about their relationship to one side. She'd had to make it work, for the baby's sake. A child needed two parents.

'I didn't mean to, I really didn't, not after what you'd just been through. I was going to wait until you were better, and then he turned up at the hospital with those stupid flowers, all concerned. *Ugh!* He looked so smug and smarmy and had the nerve to act as though nothing had happened, I just flipped. I couldn't help myself. It was a red-mist moment.'

'I'm glad you did flip.' Of course, gratitude hadn't been Fleur's response at the time, but later she had come to appreciate she had actually had a lucky escape.

She would never again let a man do to her what Adam had.

Let one try, Fleur thought, her eyes narrowing as she contemplated what she would do to any man unwise enough to attempt to locate her heart. She was no longer the hopeless romantic; her defences were totally impregnable.

* * *

He was gifted, rich, handsome and then some. If pressed to explain the secret of his success, Antonio Rochas explained there was no magic formula—he just didn't accept less than excellence from himself.

Only the previous week his face had graced the cover of no fewer than three internationally acclaimed financial journals. His reputation alone swung deals.

His reputation cut no ice with one particular female.

Antonio had been a father for a week.

He *wasn't* excelling at parenthood!

If his colleagues wondered about the source of uncharacteristic moodiness displayed by their charismatic and normally even-tempered boss during the last week, they had not done so outloud.

Huw Grant, a top-notch criminal lawyer and one of Antonio's closest friends, was less restrained.

'You don't look like a man who has just won...now *they* have reason to look less than happy,' Huw observed, watching from the privacy of the penthouse executive office suite as a trio of dark-suited figures far below left the London Rochas building. 'The poor guys came here thinking they could steal a march on you, Antonio...'

Always a fatal mistake, thought the shorter man, studying the hard lines of his friend's classically featured lean face. It occurred to him, and not for the first time, that it was infinitely preferable to be this man's friend than his enemy.

Antonio, who was sitting staring broodingly into the distance, shrugged and brushed away an invisible fleck from his impeccable jacket. 'They did not do their homework,' he observed dismissively.

'But you did...?'

The network of fine lines fanning Antonio's electric-blue

eyes deepened as his long dark lashes lifted from the slashing angle of his high cheekbones. 'I always do my homework, Huw.'

Just as he had more recently done his homework on Charles Finch.

But then when a man walked into your office and calmly announced you were the biological father of his thirteen-year-old daughter you had a lot of questions that needed answering.

He now had the answers to some of those questions, including the results of a DNA test.

According to the information that had landed on his desk, the only thing Charles Finch and his late wife had had in common was a mutual loathing and the fact they had spent more time in other people's beds than their own.

Miranda's reason for staying in the sham marriage had been obvious. As Antonio was only too well aware, she had had expensive tastes and social aspirations to match.

Charles Finch's reasons had been less immediately obvious. But then why, he mused, did people stay in bad marriages? Marriages that looked perfect on the surface, but underneath had more in common with open warfare than mutual support or love?

Presumably the other man had got something he'd needed from the twisted relationship, though what it was Antonio could not even begin to imagine.

Huw moved from the window and observed, 'And this time your homework just made you a conservative twenty million. Of course, being as ruthless as hell with no scruples to speak of helps.'

Amusement flickered in Antonio's blue eyes, eyes made more arresting by the contrasting Mediterranean colouring of his skin. 'You think I represent the ugly face of capitalism?'

'Not ugly,' the other man objected wryly.

Though if Huw's own wife was to be believed, it wasn't

just his perfect features and lean, athletic body that made women unable to take their eyes—and hands—off Antonio. It was the aura of earthy sensuality that he apparently exuded from every pore.

Not, his wife had hastily assured him, that she was affected by it.

'But you really should carry a government health warning. I mean, when was the last time someone got the better of you financially speaking? Oh, I know you're not interested in money for the sake of it,' he admitted. 'But you can't deny that you enjoy winning.'

Antonio's brows lifted. 'Doesn't everyone?'

'Well, you don't look like you do,' his friend observed frankly.

'Let's just say I have other things on my mind…' Abruptly Antonio stopped sorting files and sought the other man's eyes, then shook his head and said, 'It doesn't matter.'

'Clearly it does,' Huw said, his curiosity whetted by this uncharacteristic behaviour. 'You've been odd all week.'

Antonio leaned back in his seat and stretched his long, long legs in front of him. He rested his chin on his steepled fingers. 'You know Finch…?'

'The law firm Finch? Finch, Abbott and Ingham…Finch?' Antonio nodded.

'Cold guy. Got a really classy-looking wife, as I recall.'

'The classy-looking wife is dead,' Antonio said. Cancer, her husband had said.

Miranda was dead. Antonio still struggled with the impossible concept.

In his head she was so *alive*, her image frozen in his memory as she had been the summer he had met and fallen in love with her. He could see her laughing, her head thrown back to reveal her lovely throat. She had laughed a lot, especially when he had announced he loved her and wanted to take care of her.

'What a sweet boy you are,' she had said when she had finally realised he was deadly serious. 'Look, what we had was fun, that's all. Don't spoil it by being silly about this.'

When he persisted she was more brutal.

'Be serious—what would a woman like me want with a penniless waiter? When I get married it won't be because he's good in bed, and, darling, you really are. I can get sex anywhere. When I get married it will be to a man who can give me the life I deserve.'

Unable to interpret the edge in his friend's voice, Huw frowned. 'Bad luck. I only met him around, as you do. What's he got to do with anything?'

'He came to see me last month. It appears that his daughter isn't…'

'Isn't what?' asked Huw, looking confused.

'His. She's mine.'

CHAPTER TWO

ANTONIO almost smiled as Huw's face fell, increasing his resemblance to a startled spaniel. A resemblance that belied the criminal lawyer's sharp intellect and had lulled many an adversary into a false sense of security.

'*Yours…?*'

Antonio ran a long brown finger down the spine of a book on his desk. 'It would seem so. I have a daughter who is thirteen and she thinks I'm a monster. She tells anyone who will listen that I'm kidnapping her.'

'*Kidnapping…?*'

'Finch told her he's fighting a strenuous legal battle to get her back.'

'Get her back!' Huw exclaimed. 'What legal battle? You mean the girl is staying with you? Is that a good idea?'

A nerve in Antonio's jaw clenched as he observed grimly, 'There wasn't much time to consider the options.'

'How do you mean?'

'After he broke the *news* to me Finch explained he had Tamara waiting in the car complete with overnight bag. The rest of her things were delivered the next day. He made it pretty clear to me in private that he wants nothing more to do with her.'

'*Nothing…?*' Huw struggled with the concept.

A nerve clenched along Antonio's firm jaw. His lashes swept downwards concealing the glow of rage that lit his blue eyes. 'He never wants to see her again.'

'What a total bastard!'

Antonio could not disagree with this shocked assessment.

'A bastard who can act.' Antonio got to his feet and pushed aside his chair.

His friend watched him walk across to the window and wondered, with a touch of envy, what it would be like to effortlessly dominate any room you were in with mere physical presence.

'It was quite a performance,' Antonio admitted, looking out at the cityscape. 'Finch made a very convincing heartbroken father. The law is apparently on my side——'

'That's debatable.'

'And it seems I woke up one morning and decided to snatch the child, who *apparently* I rejected as a baby, away from her loving home.'

And Antonio had been forced to stand there and listen, unable to deny the barrage of lies without revealing the man his daughter had called Father for the past thirteen years was discarding her like a worn-out toy.

He was no psychologist, but Antonio couldn't think this would make any kid, let alone one who had recently lost her mother, feel particularly secure!

'That's what the girl thinks? No wonder she's telling people you've kidnapped her! The man's a——'

'Suffice it to say that Finch does not have a warm loving personality. I think he must have been one of those children who got their kicks pulling the wings off flies.'

'Sociopathic tendencies,' Huw inserted knowledgeably.

'If you say so.' Antonio was not really interested in labels. 'He does like to see people squirm.'

Huw frowned, unable to believe his friend was as calm as he appeared. Just imagining how such a shocking revelation would rock his own comfortable world brought him out in a cold sweat.

'Antonio, if this guy is out for revenge and he doesn't care about hurting the girl, isn't his next port of call going to be the tabloids? I know you don't give a damn what they write about you, though I still think that if you were more litigious they'd think twice, but—'

'Now there,' mocked Antonio, 'speaks a lawyer. Don't worry, there will be no story.'

Huw studied his friend's face with a frown. 'You're sure about that?'

Antonio nodded. The smile that lifted the corners of his expressive mouth did not touch his eyes. They were arctic-cold. 'Absolutely sure. Charles Finch is in no position to throw stones.'

Huw's eyes widened as comprehension dawned. 'You've got some dirt on him, haven't you?' He should have known that Antonio would already have that base covered. The other man did not leave things to chance.

'Let's just say that our Mr Finch has sailed a little close to the wind, legally speaking, on several occasions. I have often observed it is often the way with greedy men,' he remarked contemptuously.

'And he—Finch—knows you know about these indiscretions?' Huw suggested.

'I might have mentioned it,' he admitted casually.

Huw gave a sigh of relief. 'Well, that's something. Antonio, I hope you're not taking this guy's word…just because you knew his wife…?' Huw touched on the subject cautiously. Antonio was notoriously tightlipped when it came to his personal life.

Sometimes he thought that was why the tabloids' pursuit

of the wealthy Spaniard was so relentless. They simply couldn't deal with his total and, as far as Huw could tell, genuine indifference to them.

'It was before she was his wife.' Antonio, his expression unreadable, dextrously twirled a pen between his long fingers. 'Apparently she kept a diary for years, a detailed diary, which is how Finch came to discover Tamara wasn't his.'

'Being in a diary doesn't make something the truth. I kept a diary when I was a kid, it was a work of total fiction. And if you were going to invent a fictional father for your kid the rich and powerful Antonio Rochas would be a pretty good choice, don't you think?'

'This was nearly fourteen years ago. The *rich and powerful* Antonio Rochas did not exist. I was a college student pleasing my father by learning the business from the bottom up. I was working as a waiter in one of our hotels.'

'She didn't know you were the boss's son?'

'Nobody but the manager knew who I was. Besides, I just *knew* the moment I saw the girl that she was mine.'

Huw was appalled by the harsh admission. 'God, you can't rely on gut instincts, Antonio!'

'Don't worry, this isn't a total leap of faith. Finch was considerate enough to supply Tamara's DNA. I had the required tests done.'

'So there's no doubt…?'

Antonio shook his head.

'Hell I don't know what I'd do if it happened to me. What are you going to do?'

'Go back to the Grange.'

'She's there?'

Antonio nodded. 'It seemed less traumatic than dragging her back to Spain with me.' The home where his English mother had been brought up and where he had spent happy vacations as a child had passed to him on his grandfather's death. Going there had seemed a good alternative to returning home.

'Your mother's there?'

'My mother is on her world cruise,' Antonio reminded him. 'She offered to come home, but I thought it might be better if we had some time alone.' That had been eight days ago. If asked again today, Antonio was not sure his response to the maternal offer would be the same!

'Is there anything I can do…?' Huw tried not to look too obviously relieved when Antonio assured him there wasn't.

The door slammed. Antonio was beginning to suspect that his immediate future held a lot of door slamming.

There had to be a solution to this problem, he told himself. Experience had taught him there was *always* a solution.

He just didn't know what it was yet.

'You don't want me any more than I want you,' his new daughter had yelled before her dramatic exit from the room. 'You wish I don't even exist! Do you wish I hadn't been born? Stupid question—of course you do. You're not even *English*. And,' she added, glaring up into his lean dark face, 'it's *your* fault I'm so horribly tall! I got your genes!'

'I am your father.'

The gentle reminder precipitated her flight.

Hand on the door handle, she turned back, tears sparkling in her eyes.

'*Biological* father!' she sneered, making it sound like the worst insult in the world. 'And why are your eyes so blue? They're spooky…like a wolf or something with those dark rings around the iris. This place isn't my home and if anyone here calls me Miss *Rochas* again I'll scream. My name is Finch. I can't even pronounce Rochas. I hate it and I *hate* you! I wish you were dead!'

At intervals he heard the slamming of several more doors. Well, that went well.

As he looked out through the full-length Georgian windows to the green sweep of manicured lawn beyond, Tamara, her hair flying out behind her, was running as though the devil himself were on her heels.

Antonio knew that this role had been assigned to him in her eyes.

It would be dark in another hour and, though the evening was one of his favourite times to walk the woods, he was pretty sure a town-bred girl would not enjoy the experience.

On his way out, he shrugged on a jacket and shoved a torch in his pocket.

He was in luck—well, it had to happen some time—the gardener had seen her heading in the direction of the west wood. By the time he had vaulted over a stile and entered the wood the shadows were deepening and so was his concern.

Alternately calling her name and pausing to listen, he made his way deeper until finally his efforts were rewarded by suspicious rustling sounds a few hundred yards to his right, where he knew there was a clearing.

'Tamara! This is pointless. It is—' Before he had time to complete his appeal a dog, possibly the most unattractive animal he had ever seen in his life, shot out of the undergrowth blocking his path. It bared its teeth and emitted a ferocious growl.

Antonio regarded the animal with irritation rather than fear. It was small, and animals liked him—they always had.

'Clear off!' he said, using a firm, calm tone.

Animals responded well to a firm, calm tone.

Nobody had told this dog about the firm, calm tone. It carried on growling, if anything more ferociously. Ignoring the warning signs, Antonio went to move past him, at which point the animal went for his ankle. He looked down in total astonishment at it, then rolled his eyes and cursed.

Could this day get any worse?

He soon discovered that it could.

CHAPTER THREE

'HERE boy…Sandy…?' Fleur rattled the lead in her hand hopefully. Actually she didn't feel very hopeful—the light was fading fast and her hopes of finding the dog any time soon along with it.

She muttered, 'Damn,' under her breath as her jeans snagged on a bramble. A worried frown creasing the smoothness of her brow, she carefully detached her arm from the barbs of yet another aggressive bramble and rubbed the blood welling from the long scratches on her forearm. Finally abandoning her cajoling tone, she yelled.

'You stupid animal, where are you?' She had definitely had better birthdays.

One last yell and she was going home…she really was. Fleur didn't even convince herself.

Her shoulders sagged in relief when her exasperated screech was rewarded with the sound of an indistinct but definite bark. The excited canine cry seemed to come from the wooded area on a rise to her left. Stumbling a little on the uneven ground, she set off in its direction hoping that Sandy stayed put.

She turned a blind eye to another Keep Out Private Property sign—she had passed several—and entered the wooded area. Once inside she realised it was a lot denser than it had looked. Very little light managed to pierce the leafy canopy overhead and there was a lot of leafy rustling Fleur didn't like going on.

She hesitated for a moment, suddenly wondering whether if left to himself Sandy might not find his own way home, when an outbreak of agitated barking made her mutter, 'Wimp,' under her breath and, with her firmly rounded chin set, plunged into the woods proper.

About fifty yards inside the dense growth began to thin. At the same time she became aware of the human voice the dog's barking had until now masked. A male human voice. A loud, angry male voice.

Oh, my God, that's all I need.

Breathless, she burst noisily into the clearing. The figure with his back to her was dressed in jeans and a dark jacket. He was very tall, broad of shoulder and long of leg with a lean, athletic build. On his feet he wore mud-splashed leather boots; the toe of one was very close to poor Sandy.

Fleur, her protective instincts on full alert, planted her hands on her hips and said in a loud, clear voice, 'Get away from that dog this instant!'

'*Me* get away from *him*?' Despite the irritation he was feeling, Antonio's lips spasmed into an ironic grin as his gaze slewed from the snarling dog to the young woman who had flung the stern command.

As he turned his head towards her the breath caught sharply in Fleur's throat.

Oh, my good gosh! Generic his clothing might be, but there was nothing standard about that face. No wonder the paparazzi loved it. Her first thought when the shock of recognition wore off was—Jane will be pleased I found a man.

The corners of her mouth twitched into a rueful half smile.

This wasn't the sort of man Jane had had in mind, because, above all things, her best friend was a realist with an understandable—given her history—prejudice against Mediterranean males.

And men like this were extremely thin on the ground, even if you went looking for them.

Not that Fleur was looking. She didn't want a man. She blinked, felt the heat bloom in her face as his piercing, astonishingly blue gaze zeroed in on her face and thought, Especially not this man!

Not that she was going to find herself in the position of breaking the news to him that he didn't meet her requirements. Men like this were only ever seen with perfectly groomed trophy girlfriends. And she was no trophy! No trophy for a shallow, superficial billionaire playboy perhaps, but Fleur did like to think that she was the epitome of an in-control sort of person these days.

So what were the sweaty palms and pounding pulse about? As if you don't know, said the scornful voice in her head. She was mortified to feel desire clutch low in her belly as, staying a stumble away from rising panic, she forced herself to exhale the breath trapped in her throat.

If she'd known when she had woken that morning that she would meet someone who would reduce her to a mass of raging hormones she'd have stayed in bed!

I am such a coward, she decided in disgust.

In her own defence, Fleur had to admit she wasn't dealing with anything as simple as a pretty face here. She was dealing with a bucketful of raw sex appeal, and that sex appeal happened to belong to six feet five inches of lean male radiating undiluted testosterone from every gorgeous pore.

My God, he really was spectacular: golden skin, electric-blue deep set eyes, magnificent cheekbones you could cut yourself on and a mouth that was… Fleur licked her lips nervously as her reluctant but fascinated stare lingered on the mobile curve…*wow*! Even compressed into a line of impatient disapproval, his lips were indecently sensuous.

Everyone in the village had a story about him. How delightful he'd been as a young man. How since he'd inherited the manor from his grandfather he didn't stand on ceremony but just mucked in like everyone else.

Fleur had listened politely, and thought, Sure, that's *really* likely. The person they described bore little resemblance to the reputedly charismatic and ruthless entrepreneur who got almost as many column inches in the gossip pages as he did in the business pages.

And, anyhow, if he was *so* involved, how come she'd been living here for almost twelve months and she'd never set eyes on this beloved member of the community?

Until now.

'This…animal belongs to you…?'

If, while they were singing his praises, someone had touched on the subject of his extraordinary eyes and mentioned the fact that they were so blue that looking into them made a person light-headed, Fleur might have avoided the humiliating experience of being temporarily struck dumb.

Unlike the animal, Antonio noticed that its owner was not unattractive. Young, she looked barely out of her teens, long dark blond hair shaggily cut—not, he suspected, by an expert hand—surrounded an oval face. Her face was in shadow, but he could see that her mouth was soft and her eyes exotically slanted beneath the delicate curve of darkish brows.

She was dressed in jeans and what appeared to be several layers of clothing. The layers made him wonder about what was underneath. As he stared she lifted a hand to brush aside a thick strand of hair from her eyes, the knitted thing she wore hung open and the action pulled her shirt tight against the curve of her breasts. The unexpected lick of lust that travelled through his body reminded Antonio that it had been over two months since he had come out of a relationship.

'Yes, he is.' Fleur was relieved that, in contrast to the shameful sexual heat that made her skin prickle, her voice, when she regained the power of speech, was cool and composed. 'Come here, Sandy,' she said, clicking her fingers. 'Good boy,' she added coaxingly.

The dog looked at her, wagged his tail on the ground, and then went back to acting like some sort of savage beast interspersing his malevolent growls with the occasional loud, excited yap.

'*Good boy...?*' Antonio rolled his eyes skyward and wondered irritably, 'Why do people have animals they cannot control?'

One thing was certain—when he was back in a relationship again it wouldn't be with anyone who bore any resemblance to this petite blonde. No, not his type at all, and as for that wide-eyed innocent quality—did grown men *really* fall for that?

Fleur's chin went up. 'Was that question directed at me?' she asked him frostily.

'He is your animal, I take it?'

'Don't raise your voice—you'll only scare him more.'

His dark brows lifted at the sharp note of censure in her voice. Actually, it was quite an attractive voice, even when its owner was being shrewish—soft, rather deep and with an unusual sexy huskiness. It wasn't a voice that belonged to a teenager, and neither did her manner, so possibly he had misjudged her age, but then it was a long time since he had seen a woman without make-up. It probably didn't hurt that she had been blessed with flawless skin and naturally dark lashes. He caught himself wondering if her hair colour was real.

You're not going to find out, Antonio, he reminded himself.

'He does not look very scared to me,' he observed in a sardonic drawl.

Fleur, who had crouched down to entice Sandy back, slung him a tight-lipped look through the spiky fringe of dark lashes. His lashes, she noticed, were not straight but jet-black, thick and curled and ridiculously long. She found herself wondering resentfully why long lashes in a male face were so utterly irresistible?

'You *obviously* know nothing about animals.'

Did she know that he had a direct view of her cleavage? That he could see the lacy edging on her bra?

'And you *obviously* cannot read,' he snapped, thinking irritably that all work might well make for a dull boy, but in his case it made for an easily distracted one. The time he was spending looking down this woman's blouse was time that would be better spent looking for his errant daughter.

She lifted her head and he saw for the first time that her eyes were amber. He saw her realise where he was staring and flush to the roots of her hair. He hadn't been around a woman who blushed that way in a long time, if ever.

'You do know you're trespassing, I suppose?'

'Maybe your dogs can read...' Her eyes flashed angrily as she fastened another button on her shirt and gave an angry sniff.

'My dogs can respond to a command.' Pity the same couldn't be said for his libido, which, in the space of thirty seconds, had spiralled out of control.

Does that go for his women too? she wondered scornfully. He looked the type, she decided, studying his arrogant profile with a contemptuous little smile.

'Why on earth did you let him off his lead?'

Good question, and one she had been asking herself ever since he had taken off after a rabbit.

Fleur got to her feet, rubbing a weary hand across her face. 'Look, let's start again, shall we?'

'Again? You enjoyed it that much, *querida*?'

She was already scowling in response to his mocking tone; when he threw in the casual endearment her expression did a freeze-frame on tight-lipped disapproval. She could feel something unraveling—she just hoped it was her temper!

'I am sorry about the trespassing. It wasn't intentional and it won't happen again.'

'We've had a lot of trouble with poachers.'

Fleur looked at him in exasperation. 'Do I look like a poacher?' she demanded, stabbing her chest with a finger.

She actually looked soft, warm.

'I try not to stereotype; poachers come in all shapes and sizes.' So, he realised, did temptation, but then variety added a little spice to life.

Antonio was not into indiscriminate sex and he hadn't been in a position where he was forced to fight against an urge to kiss a total stranger for some time. Especially as her flea-bitten excuse for a dog had decided yet again to grab his jeans by the teeth. His resentment at finding himself in this position directed itself at the cause of his discomfort.

'I suppose you think that's funny? Well, I…' she stopped mid-rant and forced herself to smile. 'If you'd just hand Sandy back we'll be off your land…'

And not a moment too soon. With all that in-your-face, rampant maleness, he really was not a comfortable man to be around. For some women she could see how that could become a real problem, but fortunately one thing she had never had a problem with was her sexual appetite. Romance was her weakness, and she had realised a long time ago that she wasn't particularly highly sexed. And she obviously didn't give off the sort of vibes that sent men wild with lust.

'Nothing would give me more pleasure,' he revealed truth-fully. He looked at the hand extended to him, it was small, the nails unvarnished and cut short. From nowhere the idea of lifting it to his lips planted itself in his head. 'But I don't have any particular wish to lose any part of my anatomy.'

Actually it was his sanity that Antonio was more con-cerned about at that moment. Every time he looked at this woman's mouth he felt his much-vaunted self-control slip another notch.

Reminding himself that she wasn't his type worked about as well as it had the first time.

'So I'll let you remove…' The tremor that rippled through her body as he took her hand in his was visible.

Antonio stopped speaking and watched her eyes slowly lift to his. There was a shocked trance-like quality to her stare. Then as the colour ran up under her fair skin she made a tiny choking sound in her throat and snatched her hand away. She held it tight against her heaving bosom while her wide eyes stayed on his face.

He was accustomed to women looking at him, but not as though he were the embodiment of their nightmares

Fleur took a deep breath and lowered her eyes. She was utterly mortified. It would have been nice to believe that he hadn't picked up on the fact she had been virtually nailed to the spot by lustful longing. It would have been even nicer to pretend it hadn't happened at all!

Nicer, but difficult when the heat his touch had ignited still lay curled deep down in the pit of her stomach just waiting for the least excuse to burst into embarrassing flames.

Dear God, I only just stopped short of drooling! She was shaken from her reverie of self-loathing by his grunt of pain.

Antonio had momentarily forgotten about the dog, but the dog had not forgotten about him.

In reflex to the pain that shot up his leg as canine teeth broke skin Antonio straightened his knee. The jerky motion caused the dog to lose his grip. If the animal's attack had been intended to protect its mistress's virtue it had worked. The compelling urge to mesh his fingers in the blonde's hair, pull her face up to his and kiss her senseless had passed.

Fleur let out a cry of shocked outrage as the dog picked himself up from the ground.

'Why don't you pick on someone your own size, you pathetic bully?' she cried, rushing to the cringing animal. 'You're such a *big* man, aren't you?' she sneered.

Antonio Rochas, his dark head tilted to one side, appeared to be listening, but not to her. To add insult to injury he raised an impatient hand and snapped tersely, 'Silence!'

Fleur's jaw dropped. *Unbelievable!*

She had come to the conclusion he was going to ignore her totally when his gaze narrowed, which had been focused on some point beyond her, suddenly zeroed in on her face.

His long jet lashes touched the crest of his cheekbones as his glance dropped, making Fleur belatedly aware of the gaping neckline of her shirt. The blatant sexual insolence sent a shard of anger through her and something that felt like a mild electric shock.

'Who did you have in mind for me to pick on?' His expressive lips quirked as his glance slid over her outraged figure. *'You...?'*

He had never seen the attraction of women with attitude. But then he had never considered fighting foreplay—not until now, at least.

Fleur watched his lips curl into a patronising smile and gritted her teeth. She had never come across anyone whose body language screamed male arrogance this loudly.

'You shouldn't judge by appearances,' she advised darkly. 'Couldn't you see he was afraid?'

'Afraid…?' he echoed, looking at her as though she were off her head.

Straightening up with the animal in her arms, she nodded. 'Yes, afraid.' Clasping the warm, trembling body against her chest, with her free hand she brushed her hair from her face. Adam had liked it cut in a short neat bob.

She hadn't had it cut since they had split up.

Antonio arched a dark brow and reminded himself that he wasn't here to look at anyone's freshly exposed neck, even if it was just asking to be tasted. He was here to find his wayward daughter.

'I was the one being savaged by a vicious animal.'

'Savaged?' she echoed contemptuously.

'I doubt the authorities would share your attitude.'

The angry scorn on Fleur's face faded; she looked at him in horror. Under his ironic gaze a slow flush of colour rose up her neck until her face was bathed in heat. 'You can't report him,' she said in a small voice.

But he could. And he would, she thought, hating him.

'I think I would be failing in my duty not to. It might be a child the animal attacks next time.' He watched the colour seep from her face and felt like a total bastard for baiting her.

Fleur shook her head. 'No, he wouldn't do that; he loves children. It's only men he doesn't like.'

From the way she was looking at him Antonio assumed that this was a trait shared by his owner.

'He's a rescue dog. When they found him he was in a terrible state. I don't even like to think about what his owner did to make him so afraid of men. He's really a very placid animal normally. If you want to blame anyone blame me— it's my fault for letting him off the lead.'

A scream like broken glass cut across Fleur's faltering explanation. Then another and another. The sound of terror lifted the hairs on the nape of her neck.

For a moment she froze. Her companion did not; he hit the ground running. Running with a fluid animal grace and athletic co-ordination that Fleur might have admired on a more appropriate occasion.

With the sound of those screams still ringing in her ears, Fleur didn't think about *not* following him. Pausing only to attach the lead to Sandy, she plunged after him, weaving her way with far less grace than he had between the trees. My God, she thought, panting as she ran towards where the screams had come from—worryingly they had stopped— for a big man he could certainly move.

She reached the reed-fringed pond just in time to see him dive in fully clothed. His entry caused a few geese to rise squawking into the air. Eyes wide and scared, Fleur watched as he cut through the grey water with smooth, powerful strokes. It wasn't until he reached the small upturned boat that she registered its presence.

My God, she thought in horror, someone is down there.

Antonio trod water and scanned the surface. He called out, 'Tamara!' twice, then, taking a lungful of air, dived beneath the surface. At the spot the boat had overturned the pond was deep and it was hard to see anything in the murky, weed-choked depths.

The first two dives he came up empty-handed. Antonio closed his eyes and prepared to go down again. The lines of his face were set in a mask of steely determination. A calm settled over him, he knew that this time failure was simply not an option.

As the dark head vanished once more beneath the water Fleur, standing on the shore, pressed a hand to her mouth to muffle the moan of fear that escaped the confines of her dry throat.

He was fully dressed and his clothes had to weigh a ton. My God, she thought he's going to drown. I'm watching a man drown. I'm one of those awful people who stand by and do nothing!

'The stupid, *stupid* man!' At her feet the dog whined. Come up…come up… she mouthed silently as she stared at the still surface of the pond willing him to appear.

But he didn't.

Fleur jumped up and down in silent agitation. Nobody could hold their breath for that long. Damn it, she couldn't just stand here and do nothing. Slipping off her cardigan and shoes, she waded into the cold water. She was thigh-deep when his dark head broke the surface.

The ferocious tension slid from Fleur's body as her head fell back… Thank God!

CHAPTER FOUR

THERE was a raging fire where his lungs were meant to be. Antonio almost welcomed the pain that reminded him he was alive. For a moment there he had really thought that he was going to black out before he reached the surface.

It had only been the knowledge that if he didn't make it neither did Tamara that had enabled him to hold the blackness back.

He gasped greedily for air to replenish his oxygen-deprived lungs while simultaneously treading water and blinking the water from his eyes. His hand shook as he touched Tamara's cold face. Her eyelashes lay like dark curtains against the waxy grey pallor of her smooth young cheeks.

Praying harder than he had ever done in his life, he tilted her head back and breathed into her mouth…once, twice, and then again, pausing each time to feel for a pulse. His efforts were rewarded with a soft flutter under his fingers.

Rolling onto his back and supporting Tamara's body with his own, he cupped her chin, drawing her face clear of the water and, digging deep into his reserves, he kicked for shore. He had gone maybe twenty feet when he became aware of someone beside him. It was the young woman minus her dog.

'Is she breathing?'

He nodded. With her mane of hair floating in the water around her face she reminded him of an anxious mermaid. Didn't mermaids lure a man to his doom? This one seemed to be trying to help.

She swam up beside him. 'Let me…?'

Not wasting his breath on a reply, Antonio allowed her to support part of Tamara's weight. Together they swam towards the shallows towing the girl between them.

As they reached the muddy bank Antonio hefted Tamara's limp body into his arms. His eyes left his daughter's face for a second in order to say, breathlessly but imperatively, 'An ambulance.'

Following him, Fleur panted. 'I already called before…'

'Before you jumped in the lake.'

She was conscious of a tiny glow of pleasure as he flashed her a look of warm approval. Later on she was going to have to remind herself that she shouldn't want his approval, but right now there were more important things to think about.

Choosing a clear patch of grass Antonio laid down his burden.

'Tamara, can you hear me?'

In response the girl rolled onto her side and retched over and over until her stomach was empty. Antonio watched, feeling totally helpless as she then began to cry.

'I expect that was a good thing,' Fleur, her teeth chattering, observed as she retrieved the cardigan she'd pulled off before she'd gone into the water.

She dropped down onto her knees beside Antonio and, easing the shaking girl's head onto her lap, tucked the dry cardigan tight around her trembling body. It wasn't much but it was better than nothing.

'You'll be fine,' she said, hoping it was the truth. Actually the girl looked pretty awful, but the scary blue tinge around her lips had lessened.

'Tamara,' the tall Spaniard supplied huskily. 'My daughter.'

'That's a nice name,' Fleur said, rubbing the girl's cold hands in between her own. Either he was a lot older than he looked or he had started a family when he was very young. She had never heard a wife mentioned so she assumed that this girl was a child from a previous relationship.

He shook his head, sending silver water droplets spraying everywhere. 'And I am Antonio Rochas…' He ran a hand over his wet face and managed to look more vital than any man who had just had a near-death experience had a right to.

Did he really think she didn't know who he was?

'Fleur Stewart.'

She looked at him through the mesh of her wet lashes. Like hers his body was shaken by intermittent tremors, which became more obvious as he shrugged his way out of his drenched jacket.

His shirt and jeans clung like a second skin to his chest and belly, delineating his superb physique. If he had been carrying even an ounce of surplus flesh on his long, lean frame it would have shown, but it didn't and he wasn't. He was grey-hound-lean six feet five of hard male muscle. A flash of heat washed over the surface of her chilled body.

Dragging her eyes clear of the spectacle of male beauty, Fleur turned back to the distressed girl, appalled and deeply ashamed that she could notice something like lean, muscle-packed contours at a moment like this, let alone react to it. The dog beside her whined and as she absently patted him. Fleur experienced a flash of inspiration.

'Come here, Sandy,' she encouraged, holding out her hand.

'What are you doing?'

'That's it, good boy,' she crooned approvingly to the dog as he curled up beside the girl. 'Sandy's warm and she's cold. I'd offer her my body heat but I don't think I have any.'

'Good dog,' he said.

'Be careful!' Fleur stopped as to her amazement her man-hating pet licked the male fingers that tickled his ears. 'Fickle animal.'

The complaint made his lips twitch, but a moment later his forehead was creased with worry as he looked down at Tamara. 'Perhaps I should take her back to the house. When you rang you told the emergency services our location…?'

'Yes, of course.'

His eyes narrowed as he visualised the route they would take. 'They'll come along the track from the house,' he predicted, looking with a frown around the tree-fringed clearing. 'We should get out of here and meet them there.'

Fleur nodded. 'That makes sense,' she admitted. The change in his manner now that he had a purpose was noticeable.

It was obvious to Fleur that Antonio Rochas was not the type of person who enjoyed sitting back waiting for things to happen. He was the sort of man who made things happen and relished being in charge of a situation…definitely *not* a relaxing person to be around.

But then maybe not relaxing worked. She had never read a financial page in her life and even Fleur knew that people who knew about such things spoke his name with awe and envy.

The Rochas family name had already been synonymous with the international hotel group of the same name, but after this man had taken over the firm after his father's death it had broadened its scope, acquiring amongst other things an airline and a newspaper.

All were now incredibly successful.

'I don't want...' the girl began fretfully as her father scooped her up into his arms.

'Right now I don't much care what you want, Tamara. *Madre mía,* what were you doing going out in that boat anyway when you can't swim?'

'I c...can swim. I lost the oar and I was trying to reach it when I fell in. There were reeds and stuff in the bottom—my leg got stuck.'

'She's upset; there's no need to be so brutal,' Fleur admonished. 'After an experience like that—'

'After an experience like that,' he cut in grimly. 'it's to be hoped she has learnt her lesson. But based on past experience I don't think I'll hold my breath.'

'You poor thing...it's all right now,' Fleur soothed as the girl started weeping. Noticing for the first time the lines of strain bracketing her father's overtly sensual mouth, Fleur realised that the girl wasn't the only one who had had a bad experience.

It didn't take long for them to exit the wooded area. The only problem with being in the open was that it was more exposed to the elements. The wind was light but it cut through Fleur's wet clothes with the viciousness of a sharp blade.

The minutes ticked by and Antonio began to pace up and down pausing intermittently in order to stare impatiently up the track. He reminded Fleur irresistibly of a sleek caged jungle cat, so graceful to watch that it almost hurt.

'Where are they...?' He angled an accusing glare at Fleur.

'Don't worry, they'll be here soon,' she soothed, tolerant of being spoken to as if it were her fault only because she recognised his aggression for what it was. He was worried sick about his daughter.

'Don't worry!' he echoed. 'This is my daughter lying here!

Do you have any idea—' He broke off and, jamming both hands into his saturated hair, let his head fall forward.

Fleur listened to the harsh sound of his laboured breathing and her throat ached with sympathy.

Frowning, Antonio lifted his head and scanned her face. The indentation above his masterful nose deepened. 'Do you have a child?'

The unexpected question made Fleur stiffen. She made a mental note that his perception was uncomfortably acute and shook her head. 'No, I don't.'

Before Antonio had an opportunity to wonder about the stricken expression he had glimpsed in her wide-spaced eyes he heard the sound of an engine. Relief swept over him. A moment later the ambulance came into view.

'I'm c-cold.'

Fleur, who could readily identify with the girl's complaint, watched as her father dropped gracefully down on his knees beside her. 'Don't worry,' he soothed, taking her hands between his. 'The ambulance is here. You'll be fine now.' He laid a hand on her shoulder and felt her flinch.

The ambulance team were smooth and efficient. Fleur stood back to let them get on with their job. Antonio joined her, his expression grave as he watched the men strap his daughter to a stretcher.

After they had loaded their patient the paramedic stood to one side to let Antonio enter the ambulance.

'No! I don't want him in here.' The youthful voice rose as she added in obvious agitation, 'Make him go away! I won't have him near me. He's not my father.'

'I am her father.'

Nobody argued with him.

'No, he's kidnapped me! I want to go home, I want my real dad!'

A tense silence followed this startling and vitriolic outburst.

Fleur watched the medic direct a cautious look at Antonio, who stood there looking as flexible as a rock face. The man then exchanged a look with his partner. A look that seemed to say, If he wants to get in, there's not a lot we can do to stop him.

He cleared his throat and offered a tactful smile. 'It might be better not to…she's—' he began.

'I understand,' Antonio cut in. 'I will follow.' His expression was blank as he stepped away from the door.

The other man looked relieved.

Antonio's expression remained inscrutable as they closed the doors and drew away, lights flashing, but Fleur was assuming that he'd had better days.

Drawing the blanket the ambulance driver had given her when she had promised him she didn't need medical attention around her shoulders, Fleur shivered.

Her tall companion, who continued to stared fixedly into the distance, remained oblivious to the fact she was one step away from hypothermia. She had a strong suspicion he had forgotten she was there. Which, given what had just passed, was hardly surprising.

She told herself it was none of her business. But of course she was curious—who wouldn't be…?

Finally she couldn't keep quiet any longer. She was losing feeling in her fingers. She cleared her throat. 'That was quite a rescue.'

At the sound of her voice he spun around.

For a brief moment his expression was unveiled. The awful bleakness she glimpsed in his eyes was so shocking that Fleur actually found herself feeling sorry for him, which, considering the fact just looking at him made her skin crawl with antipathy—and other things, but she didn't want to go there— was nothing short of amazing.

'If you lose all your money you'd make a very good life-guard.'

His incredible electric-blue eyes narrowed. 'You're still here,' he said flatly.

It was always good, she thought wryly, to make an impression.

'Where did you think I'd gone?' The spasmodic clenching of the muscles along his strong jaw line was the only clue that he wasn't quite as together as he looked. He really did have an incredible face, she thought with an inward sigh of appreciation as she admired bone structure that was simply sublime.

'I suppose it's difficult being a part-time father.'

'I am not a part-time father.'

No but you are a total pain. Still, he was having a bad day. 'When I was a kid, and I was mad with my parents, I used to fantasise that I was adopted.'

He turned his head; his blue eyes were flat and unfriendly as they fixed on her. 'Is that meant to offer me comfort?' The sardonic contempt in his cold smile made her feel totally stupid for caring.

She *was* totally stupid for caring.

'Don't worry, it won't happen again,' she promised grimly. 'It's none of my business that your daughter hates you.'

Perhaps he should smile at the girl more, Fleur thought, recalling that fleeting moment when she had been on the receiving end of his approval. A smile like that was a definite unfair advantage, a weapon. Which begged the question: why didn't he use it instead of resorting to caustic comments and dark scowls?

'I do not like people who interfere in my affairs.'

'Then I'll just have to learn to live without your love…a blow,' she admitted, determined to establish herself as hard and uncaring. 'But those, as they say, are the breaks.'

He ignored her sarcasm and studied her face for a moment. Then to her surprise some of the hauteur died from his expression. 'Just keep out of my head, little girl.'

'Believe me, it's one of the last places I would want to go.'

One side of his mouth quirked into an almost-smile. 'You look cold.'

And you look almost human. 'I thought you'd never notice.' Fleur clenched her chattering teeth and wished she shared his indifference to the cold. 'The blue tinge is the clue.' Just how cold did you have to get before hypothermia set in?

'I must get to the hospital to be with Tamara.' He slid her an assessing look. 'If you can keep up with me someone will get you dry things and give you a ride home. Or if you prefer I will have the Range Rover sent back for you.'

'I can keep up. And so can he,' she said, nodding to the dog who sat curled up at his feet.

Antonio looked openly sceptical of her claim. 'Well, if you can't don't expect me to wait for you,' he warned.

Fleur smiled as though a hike in wet clothes was just the sort of challenge she enjoyed on her birthday. 'And I won't wait for you,' she promised.

She soon discovered that he had really meant it when he had said he wasn't making any concessions. Fleur had to quite literally jog to keep up with him. Five minutes later when the lights of the Grange came into view she was panting.

As the house was hidden from the public road down a mile-long private drive this was the first time she had seen it. It was not what she had expected.

'I thought it would be older.' The sprawling building she was looking at was large and impressive, but it didn't seem especially ancient.

'The original house dated back to the fifteenth century; it burnt down at the turn of the century. All that's left of the old house are the cellars. The present house was commissioned by my mother's grandfather,' Antonio explained as he waited with obvious impatience for her to negotiate a rocky outcrop.

Fleur fell behind as he covered the last hundred metres and by the time she walked through the impressive front door Antonio was already running up the curved staircase that dominated the entrance hall.

It was all a bit of a blur. There were lights everywhere, he was yelling in two languages and people were scurrying.

A middle-aged woman urged Fleur towards the sweeping staircase and said with a smile, 'I'll be right with you.'

A very short time later Fleur was still standing there in the echoey yet thankfully warm hallway when Antonio reappeared, rubbing his wet sable hair with a towel. He had obviously dressed in a hurry—the leather belt of his jeans was unfastened and his shirt hung open.

She swallowed, her eyes drawn irresistibly to the exposed golden flesh. Averting her eyes quickly—but not quickly enough to prevent her stomach muscles from going crazy—she cleared her throat.

He noticed her, frowned, and then looked annoyed. 'Why has no one attended to you?'

'I expect they were busy.' Busy responding to the steady stream of instructions he had issued as he had athletically bounded up the stairs.

'*Busy…?*' he repeated with a displeased frown. 'This is totally unacceptable…' He looked around the deserted hallway and raised his voice.

'Mrs Saunders!'

Great projection. Great voice too, if you like husky velvet with that sexy foreign inflection and, let's face it, who wouldn't? Her restless gaze returned of its own volition to his taut belly ridged by muscle and textured with a light sprinkling of dark hair. She swallowed as a lustful lick of heat warmed the centre of her chilled body—actually great everything!

'Mrs Saunders!'

'My God, I'm glad I don't work for you.' Especially if he made a habit of walking around semi-clothed, she thought, studying the painting above his head.

He turned his head and gave a sardonic smile. 'On this subject we are in total agreement.'

'Look, you go,' she encouraged. Or at least put on some more clothes. 'There's absolutely no point hanging around. All I need is a dry set of clothes and my dog back, if that is possible,' she added, directing a wry glance towards the animal at his feet. 'Traitor,' she inserted reproachfully as she shook her head.

She was going to have to have a quiet word with that faithless hound and explain the facts of life to him. Antonio Rochas wouldn't look twice at a dog without a pedigree any more than he would look twice at a woman who lacked catwalk good looks. For people like him appearances were everything. The sudden realisation that she was displaying the exact characteristics she was condemning him for drew a husky laugh from her throat.

Covering her mouth with her hand, she looked up and found he was watching her.

'It's nothing,' she provided. 'I was just thinking…'

'Happy thoughts, it would seem.'

'Not exactly. Look, why don't you just get along to the hospital? I'll be fine. I hope your daughter makes a full recovery.' Hopefully her nervous system would do the same once he was safely out of the way.

Antonio inclined his head in response and was actually turning away when he froze. Inexplicably he appeared to be studying the floor.

Under his tan he had gone pale.

'What's wrong?'

'What's wrong?' he asked, looking at her incredulously. 'You're standing in a pool of blood.'

CHAPTER FIVE

'NOT a *pool*,' Fleur protested the exaggeration. 'And it's mostly water,' she promised with a rueful glance downwards. 'The carpet should come clean; professional cleaners can work miracles these days.'

'The carpet! Why would I care about the carpet?'

'Well, I'm no expert,' she admitted, using both hands to lift the heavy weight of her wet hair from her neck as she studied the weave beneath her feet. 'But it looks like an Aubusson to me and…'

Antonio ground his teeth and laid his hands on her shoulders. Through the wet fabric of her shirt he was aware of the shape of her bones and the shocking chill of her skin.

'If you say another word I will strangle you.' Kissing her, inserting his tongue between her soft lips and sampling the sweet softness within would be an equally efficient method of silencing her. But, he suspected, much more dangerous.

A man could start kissing that mouth and find himself unable to stop. A man whose daughter lay in a hospital bed should not even be thinking such thoughts.

Fleur found that his unblinking blue stare had a strangely hypnotic quality. He sounded as if he meant the strangling part. A sensible person should at this point feel scared, or angry, or both. Instead she was thinking about his eyes and the way he smelt of warm, clean male.

Maybe I hit my head as well as my leg…? It would be an explanation for the strange thoughts that kept popping unbidden into her head.

Satisfied he had her attention, Antonio continued, the rasp in his deep voice external evidence of his inner struggle not to lose it big time.

'You are injured.' Not to mention unhinged. He looked at the lush softness of her mouth and thought, Which makes two of us.

'Just a little scratch.' I hope. 'You know a little bit of blood can look like a lot, especially when it's mixed with half a gallon of water. It really isn't a big thing.'

His fingers tightened on the skin that covered her delicate collar-bones. *'You knew!'*

Fleur winced and he lifted his hands, holding them palm upright towards her. 'Sorry, did I hurt you?' His glance drifted down her body. There was an uncharacteristic vagueness in his shadowed blue eyes as they returned to her face. 'You look so delicate.'

The observation emerged sounding very like an accusation.

'I'm tougher than I look,' she promised him.

'Not so tough you did not notice until now you'd injured yourself.' He thought of the direct route he had taken back to the house, a route that even the most committed hill-walker would have found tough, and she hadn't asked for help once.

This woman took stubborn into uncharted territory, along with his temper.

'Well, I felt *something* when I was in the water,' she admitted, wrinkling her nose as she recalled the sharp pain in her leg when she had been swimming out to him. 'But I forgot about it.' There had after all been a lot else to think about.

Antonio's exasperation and temper climbed to breaking

point. 'Why in God's name did you not say something? Are you a martyr or an idiot?'

'Neither,' she protested indignantly. 'The water was cold, I suppose I was numb, and, like I said, I forgot about it.' She wished she were still numb. Since they had come indoors the throbbing pain in her leg had become painfully intrusive.

'*Forgot!* Give me strength,' he gritted, rolling his eyes heavenwards. 'We're wasting time here.'

'I'm not—'

'I don't want to hear it!' he blasted. 'Just tell me where you are injured and we will take it from there.'

'You need to get to the hospital.'

'Yes, I do. So just answer my question and stop wasting my time.'

Fleur sighed and reluctantly gestured towards her right thigh, careful not to touch the painful area.

'Right, take off those jeans and let me have a look.'

Fleur saw an image in her head of his hands dark against the skin of her inner thigh and a jolt of sexual longing slammed through her body. Even as she stood there trying to banish the images she saw his mouth replace his fingers—in fact she could practically feel it!

'I'm not taking off my jeans.' She caught herself trying to remember which pants she had put on that morning and, flushing, shook her head. 'I'm definitely not taking off my jeans.' Modest white cotton with rosebuds...pink rosebuds.

'If you don't, I will. Yes,' he said, smiling wolfishly into her shocked face, 'you're right; I would. And spare me the false modesty,' he begged.

'It's really not necessary.' Even as she spoke she knew the protest was useless. One thing Antonio Rochas did *not* come across as was a man to be diverted once he'd made up his mind about something.

'Let me decide what is necessary, because if you bleed to death on my premises it will be me who will be held responsible.'

'So you're covering yourself and here was me thinking you cared,' she trilled sarcastically. 'Relax, Mr Rochas, you're not responsible for me…and there's no need to swear,' she added with a disapproving sniff.

He looked at her mouth and thought about other ways he could release his feelings. Inhaling through flared nostrils, he pressed the heel of one hand to his forehead and told her, 'You are enough to make a saint swear.'

'Something nobody is about to accuse you of if the stuff I've read is even half true.'

'How exciting for you,' he drawled sarcastically. 'After reading the thrilling instalments of my life in the pages in your intellectually stimulating magazines you're actually experiencing a day in my life firsthand.' He angled an enquiring brow. 'Are you enjoying it?'

'Strangely enough, no. And please don't insult me by lumping me together with your *adoring* fans.' Poor misguided women all. 'I admit I have seen your photo and even read a few lines about your charmed existence in the dentist or hairdresser's…but I found it neither thrilling nor particularly interesting,' she fired back.

'I'm surprised,' he admitted.

'Because I can read?'

'I'm surprised that you know what the inside of a hairdressing salon looks like.'

'*Very funny*…I suppose the women you know never have a hair out of place.' Except when he made love to them. Appalled by the maverick thought, Fleur, her hands curled into tight fists, allowed her eyelashes to flicker downward in a protective screen.

Antonio thought of the women in his life, each one poised, elegant, guaranteed to handle themselves in any company and all groomed to within an inch of their lives.

'No, they don't.' His flickering glance touched to the tousled head of the woman who tilted her head to glare contemptuously up at him. A smile tugged at the corners of his mouth. 'But then neither would they leap into a lake to rescue someone they didn't even know. I don't think I've thanked you—that was a very brave thing to do.'

The totally unexpected compliment threw Fleur totally. She took refuge in flippancy. 'I was after the reward.'

'The pleasure of my company?' he suggested. 'No, don't answer that,' he pleaded quickly. 'I'm not sure my ego will take any more bashing.'

'Oh, I think it would survive a force-five hurricane. You know,' she said injecting a note of discovery into her saccharine-laced voice, 'if you took away your vanity, egoism and overly high opinion of yourself you wouldn't have any personality at all.'

For a second she saw shock register in his eyes, but it was swiftly subsumed by amusement and, rather to her alarm, interest. 'I have a confession...I have never had so much trouble getting a woman to take off her clothes for me.'

The husky rasp of his voice had an effect on every single nerve ending in her body. The horror on her face was very real as she begged hoarsely, 'Spare me the details!' Her over-stimulated imagination was already providing plenty of those.

The things going on in her head made it hard for Fleur to look him in the face. If he guessed she would die of shame...

'Let's just hope your reputation doesn't suffer lasting damage,' she said, lacing her words with as much insincerity as she could.

Frustratingly the acid jibe just made him grin some more

and ask, 'What's your problem anyway?' He studied her stubborn expression and produced a possible explanation. 'Are you not wearing underclothes or something?'

Fleur, her mind still dealing with a number of erotic mental images involving women stripping for his pleasure, felt mortified colour fly to her face.

'Of course I'm wearing knickers!' A discussion of her underwear or possible lack of with Antonio Rochas...could this day get any more surreal?

'Then the sooner you stop behaving like a petulant child and take off those jeans, the sooner I can get to the hospital to see my daughter.'

At that moment the middle-aged woman from earlier appeared. 'I am so sorry, miss, I was so long, but—' She stopped dead when she saw Antonio.

He turned his head. 'You have dry clothes, Mrs Saunders?'

'Some towels and a robe.'

Fleur smiled and said, 'That's very kind. I'll be fine now with Mrs Saunders...'

'Mrs Saunders has more important things to attend to,' he cut in smoothly. 'If you could get me some surgical tape and a dry dressing?' He opened the door to Fleur's right and took the bundle from the older woman before turning back to Fleur. 'Come on, I haven't got all day.'

'Which charm school did you graduate from?' she asked him sweetly as, left with little choice, she followed him into the room. Hovering in the doorway, she slid a curious glance around the bedroom. It was decorated in a feminine style in shades of lilac with sprigged wallpaper and a four-poster bed.

'My sister's,' he said, watching her. 'It was,' he revealed with an expressive grimace, 'her lilac period. Nowadays she and her husband, along with their litter of kids, take a suite in the west wing, but whenever decorating this room is suggested she comes down with a bad case of nostalgia.'

Fleur continued to hover as he dragged a chair that stood against the wall towards her. His attitude was impatient as he instructed her to, 'Take off the jeans and take a seat.' He stood there, his arms folded across his bare chest, shoulders braced against the wall.

She nibbled on her lower lip. Logically she knew that prolonging this and making a big thing of it was only going to make her look more of a fool than she already did. The knowledge did not affect her reluctance. Exhaling a gusty sigh, she lifted her chin and shrugged as if the problem were his, not hers.

Her hands were shaking as she unfastened the button on her jeans and fumbled with the zip. Sliding the fabric down her hips, she stood there feeling horribly exposed and totally ridiculous. She sat on the chair he had provided and eased the jeans lower until they reached her ankles.

'I thought the secret of success was the ability to delegate…?' she grumbled as he dropped down to his knees beside her.

His head lifted. He was so close she could see the gold tip to each individual eyelash. It made sense that if she could smell the soap he'd just showered with he could smell her fear. *Fear…?* Dear God, I'm going crazy. There's no reason in the world for me to be afraid of Antonio Rochas.

And then it hit her, the truth—she wasn't afraid of Antonio Rochas. She was afraid of the way he made her feel… She inhaled deeply. She was afraid of *feeling*!

It was one revelation she could have done without.

She turned her head as he scanned the injured area. His attitude was clinical and his light touch objective…an objectivity she wistfully envied.

'Tell me if I hurt you.'

Fleur gave a noncommittal grunt.

His dark brows knit into a frown as he concentrated. 'Relax!' he ordered tersely.

If only it were that easy, she thought, looking at the top of his dark head. Almost immediately she found herself fighting a compelling need to sink her fingers into the glossy wet strands.

She closed her eyes and took a deep sustaining breath. The sooner she put as much space between herself and this man, the sooner she could get back to normality!

After a moment—it seemed a lot longer to Fleur—he gave his verdict. 'It's deep.' It was still oozing blood and the area around the jagged tear in her smooth flesh was red, inflamed and angry-looking. It had to be hurting like hell.

'But not life-threatening.' She gave a nervous laugh, then winced as his fingers lightly brushed the sensitive skin of her thigh.

'That depends on whether you intend to get it treated.' Balanced on the balls of his feet, Antonio rested his hands on his thighs and angled a critical look at her face.

If I tried that, she thought, I'd fall flat on my face.

'You look feverish,' he observed critically.

'I'm not feverish. Anyone,' she accused, 'would think you *wanted* me to be ill.' This time her laugh just stopped short of hysterical. 'Well, if you've seen enough,' she added, lifting her bottom from the seat and yanking the jeans upwards. The fabric caught against the injured area and she winced, tears of pain filling her eyes.

'You'll start it bleeding again, you little idiot,' he said, catching hold of her hand.

The protest shrivelled on her tongue as Fleur stared at the long brown fingers curled around her own. She touched the tip of her tongue to her dry lips. Her heart was banging so hard against her ribs that he should have been able to hear it.

'Besides, you need to get into dry clothes,' he added, easing her jeans carefully back down to her ankles.

She looked at the top of his sleekly wet head, felt her pulses quicken and thought, What I *need* is for you not to be here.

'Are you covered for tetanus?'

'I've no idea.'

The admission earned her a scornful look, but Fleur barely noticed. She shifted restlessly in the chair, and pondered some more the worrying discovery that the lightest and most clinical touch of his brown fingers could make her ache deep inside. She looked at the dark shadow of his jaw and caught herself wondering how it would feel to be kissed by a man with stubble.

These were very dangerous thoughts for a girl who had sworn off men, but then Antonio Rochas, she reminded herself—it might sink in at some point—was a very dangerous man.

'I should think you'll need a few stitches and probably antibiotics.'

Great! Her day was complete. Stitches equated doctors and the hateful smell of hospitals. 'No way.'

Impatience coloured his voice as he suggested laconically, 'Shall we let the doctors decide that?'

His tone set her teeth on edge. 'The women in your life may enjoy being patronized, but I don't,' she informed him tartly. 'I mean it—I'm not going to the hospital.' The last time she had lost her baby.

'You would prefer to bleed to death, or be permanently scarred…?' he suggested.

Fleur drew a shaky breath as she dragged herself back to the present. 'I don't care about scars.' To a man to whom appearances probably meant everything this probably sounded strange. 'I'll stick a plaster on it.'

'What about infection? Do you embrace that so joyously too?' he wondered sarcastically. 'That water was hardly a sterile environment.'

She peered down at the cut on her leg and was quite shocked by what she saw. 'It looks worse than it is,' she protested weakly.

'You can wheel out as many clichés as you like, it'll still need more than a sticking plaster.'

'You really think it'll need stitching…?'

'I'm not a doctor, but, yes, I think so.'

'Right.'

'Is that a right you'll stop being obstructive? Or a reference to my lack of medical credentials?'

Mutely Fleur nodded. 'I'll go…I'm not very…' her eyes slid from his '…not terribly…I don't like hospitals much.'

He looked at her keenly but only shrugged and said, 'Who does?'

At that moment the housekeeper returned carrying a box, which Fleur presumed held the items he had requested.

She grimaced as she saw the gaping wound and said sympathetically, 'Oh, my, that does look painful.'

'Not really.'

'Very stiff upper lip,' Antonio interrupted. 'No, thank you, Mrs Saunders, I'll do it. Could you ask John to bring the Mercedes around to the front? We'll go straight off to the hospital.'

With a smile in Fleur's direction the woman excused herself.

'I'd prefer you let your housekeeper do this,' Fleur said as she watched him extract a dressing pad and some tape from the box.

'Don't worry, I can cope with a dry dressing. I'll be gentle,' he promised when she remained silent.

It wasn't his level of competence she was concerned about, and what really worried her most was the suspicion he knew that.

Antonio was actually as proficient as he had claimed. In a

matter of moments he had covered the area with a clean dry dressing and secured it with tape.

'Fine, that's done,' he said, leaning back on his heels and surveying his handwork.

It was actually a bit of an anticlimax. She barely even needed to call on the breathing technique she had been taught in her yoga class.

'Thanks,' she said, getting to her feet. As she pulled up her wet jeans he walked over to the wardrobe.

'Try this,' he suggested, pulling something off a hanger and tossing it to her.

Fleur automatically caught it. It was a cotton tee shirt. A pair of trousers landed at her feet a moment later.

'My sister's. You can't stay in those wet things.'

Only too aware of the wet fabric chafing her skin, Fleur could not disagree.

However, she made no attempt to pick them up—just stood there.

'I can't find any underclothes, I'm afraid.' His narrowed eyes moved in a casual assessing sweep over her slim body. 'And I doubt if Sophia's would fit you anyway.'

Fleur's response to his scrutiny was anything but casual. She felt a compulsion to cover herself with her hands, but instead she lifted her chin and stared at him with what she hoped passed for cool defiance.

It was Antonio who finally broke the nerve-shredding silence.

'I suppose you expect me to turn my back…?' he observed, sounding amused.

'No, I expect you to leave the room,' she retorted, trying to inject as much dignity into her words as a person who looked like a drowned rat could.

She didn't expect him to comply with her edict. When he did she felt weak with relief.

The moment he was out of the room she began to tear off what remained of her sodden clothes. The possibility of him walking in when she was practically naked made her perform the task with feverish speed.

Fleur had just pulled the loose-fitting trousers, which were several inches too long, over her hips when she happened to catch a glimpse of herself in the full-length cheval-mirror. She stopped dead, one hand still holding her hair back from her face, the other anchoring the waistband of the trousers, and let out an anguished groan of horror.

The fine silky tee shirt had been intended for a woman with a lot less up top than she had. It clung in a positively indecent way to her unfettered breasts.

'Oh, my, I look like a…' Fleur never got to voice the uncomplimentary comment.

'I was wondering what was underneath the layers…now I know.'

Antonio had used his time outside the room to ring the hospital. The doctor he had spoken to had been reassuring— to quote him, 'She was a very lucky girl; she'll be fine.' It was Antonio who felt he was lucky; he had been given a second chance.

Filled with a new sense of purpose and buoyed by the news that Tamara was in no danger, he'd actually been able to feel the tension leave his spine as he had walked back into the room.

But one look at Fleur and he no longer felt relaxed or anything even closely related.

Fleur spun around so fast the unconsidered action sent a stab of pain shooting up her injured leg.

Wincing, she bent forward, her hand pressed to her mouth.

'You little idiot!'

'Thanks for the sympathy vote,' she snapped as she straightened up.

'Are you all right?'

She pushed the damp strands of hair from her eyes and found he wasn't looking at her leg, but her breasts. Her lips tightened and she brought up her crossed hands in a protective gesture, hating the fact she had no more control over the hot colour that flooded her cheeks than she did her quivering stomach muscles.

'Do you mind?'

His heavy-lidded eyes lifted, the predatory glitter in his cerulean eyes cancelling out his amused smile. For a moment they stood, their eyes meshed.

Then without a word he walked across to a chest. After opening several drawers he pulled out a cream cashmere cardigan. 'Try this,' he suggested.

Fleur, her eyes lowered, took it, and hoped the fact she had taken the utmost care not to let her fingertips graze his was not too obvious. By the time she had fought her way awkwardly into it her heart rate, if not normal, at least allowed her to breathe fairly normally.

If she had been given the option of jumping into an icy lake for the second time that day or getting into a car—an enclosed space—with this man there was no contest. She would opt for the lake every single time!

Only she wasn't being offered that option, so the best she could hope for was that she didn't make it too obvious that her hormones were totally out of control around him.

CHAPTER SIX

'YOU know I really don't like leaving him,' Fleur fretted.

Antonio took a deep breath. They were not at the bottom of the drive yet and she had mentioned the animal three times. This did not bode well for the journey.

'Your dog will be fine,' he told her, sounding fatigued. 'I have given strict instructions that no *male* is to go anywhere near him.'

'But—'

'No buts!'

This autocratic decree brought Fleur's chin up.

'Anyway, you *know* the animal will be fine.'

As far as Fleur was concerned to have her concern so summarily dismissed was just another example of this man's total egocentricity.

'You can frown at me,' he said without diverting his attention from the road, 'but you know I am right. You have created a problem, and fixated on it, basically because you don't want to think about what is really bothering you.' His blue gaze briefly brushed her face. 'I suppose hospital phobias are not uncommon.'

As he turned his attention back to the road ahead Fleur studied his profile with some alarm, glad that on this occasion at least his instincts had failed him. Having Antonio Rochas realise that she was almost equally worried about spending time alone with him as she was nervous about going to the hospital would be deeply embarrassing.

She didn't even know why she felt that way. It wasn't that she expected him to leap on her or anything.

It was the fact she might *want* him to that had her scared out of her mind. She wondered whether his raw masculinity affected all women this way…

She slanted him an unfriendly look. 'I don't have a hospital phobia—I just don't like hospitals. If you want to spend the journey delving into my psyche feel free, but I have to tell you you're not very good at it.'

'I'm more concerned about my daughter than your tortured psyche.'

Fleur grimaced, aware that she deserved the rebuke. 'Of course you are. I'm sorry.'

The unstinting apology drew a quick sideways glance from him, but no comment. As his electric eyes brushed her own, Fleur's outstretched hand stilled above his thigh.

'I'm sure she'll be all right.' Crazy enough she felt the need to offer him comfort even though it was clearly not required, but squeezing Antonio's *thigh*…?

'I appreciate your attempt to be supportive,' he observed with silky sarcasm, 'but believe me when I say I'd find silence infinitely preferable.'

'Fine, that suits me perfectly,' she bit back. 'I was only trying to be…' She bit her lip. 'I won't say another word.' Then when he said nothing she added, 'Look, when I'm nervous I talk.' She glared at his smug I-told-you-so profile and gritted, 'You don't have to listen. Tune me out.'

'Believe me, if I could I would. Your voice is…'

'My voice is what? It grates on you? Is it too shrill, too

loud…?' She pitched her voice an octave lower and introduced a low sexy rasp as she asked, 'Would you prefer I giggled or—?' She stopped dead and closed her eyes. 'Will you listen to me? You're right,' she confessed, holding up her hands in mock surrender, and let him believe the least humiliating of her two present concerns. 'I think I must have a hospital phobia.' What she did have was just as irrational as any phobia.

'And a very sexy voice.'

The dry aside made her stiffen and slant a suspicious look in his direction. 'And awful hair,' she reminded him.

'I didn't say it was awful,' he said, looking at the road and thinking about pushing his fingers into that lush, shiny mass, letting the silky strands slide like water through his fingers.

'Adam would,' she mused, a distant expression on her face as she absently twirled a strand. 'He'd hate it. He liked my hair short and neat.' And I listened to him. I cut my hair; I lengthened my skirts; I allowed him to make me look stupid in front of his friends. What does that make me?

'Who is Adam?' He was conscious of her stiffening before she replied in a voice that was wiped clean of all emotion.

'I was engaged to him.' She supposed the thing about repressive relationships was that you didn't even begin to suspect you had been in one until you had escaped.

Antonio's eyes slid to her slim finger. 'Past tense…?'

She nodded. 'Yes, these days I don't have to ask anyone's permission to cut my hair.'

'You don't look like a woman who asks permission for anything.'

Her shocked eyes brushed briefly with his before she lowered them and he turned his attention back to the road.

'I'm not,' she said after a moment. 'I just forgot it for a while.' She swallowed to relieve the emotional constriction in her throat.

'It happens,' he agreed. In his experience you scratched the surface of the average control freak and you revealed a pathetic loser riddled with insecurities. 'You lived with this Adam?'

She wondered how far it was to the hospital and considered telling him to mind his own business, and then thought, What did it matter? It wasn't as if it were a secret or anything.

'Yes, for nearly three years. We split up about eighteen months ago.'

'Madre di Dios! How old were you when you moved in?'

'Is that relevant?' she countered spikily. 'I was twenty...so what? People can be just as stupid when they're thirty as they are when they're twenty.'

'Twenty?' His breath escaped in a hissing sigh of disbelief. *Insane!* My daughter will be twenty in seven years' time.' The realisation hit him like a ton of bricks falling on his chest.

'She's going to be a knockout when she's older,' Fleur predicted. 'You're going to have trouble long before she's twenty.'

As images of men with evil intentions pursuing his little girl flashed through Antonio's mind he felt the foundations of his once-stable world shift even farther.

'I don't think so.' The present was so bad it had not occurred to him that there was every chance that the future could be worse.

'Oh, you're of the over-my-dead-body school of thought?' Fleur mocked.

His jaw tightened. 'I believe in discipline.'

'You do know the surest way to send a female into the arms of an unsuitable man is to offer opposition?'

The little witch is patronising me! His eyes, fixed on the road ahead, narrowed. 'Didn't your parents have anything to say when you moved in with this man?'

'I was a very mature twenty...' And her parents had at that point just retired to Scotland.

'And now you're a very *mature*, damaged…what twenty-four?'

'Twenty-five.' Her eyes widened as she recalled it was her birthday. 'Today, actually.' Her head turned as a frown formed on her smooth brow. 'And I am not *damaged*!' she yelled, her voice very loud in the confines of the car. 'Or do you think anyone who isn't an innocent virgin *damaged goods*? What century are you living in?'

'I was speaking about emotional damage.'

'Well, don't, because it's not any of your business,' she growled.

'For the record, I have no especially strong feelings about virgins.'

'How emotionally mature of you.'

'Would this be the right moment to wish you a happy birthday? I don't suppose that this was the way you planned to spend it.'

'Nobody *plans* a day like today; they just have nightmares about it.'

'Well, you'll never forget it, at least.'

Or you. 'Just like chicken pox.' She lowered her eyes, which currently had a disturbing tendency to drift towards his profile.

'Did you have something special arranged?' Was some man waiting for her with flowers and champagne? 'Now I understand your crankiness. I suppose I should apologise for spoiling your plans.'

'I am not cranky! And…I was just having a quiet night in.'

'*Alone…?*'

Fleur flushed, aware that she was in danger of appearing like a sad loser if she told him what her plans for her birthday had been. 'What is this—twenty questions? You're getting my life history and I don't know anything about you.'

'I thought reading those magazines had made you an expert.'

'I suppose there might have been one or two things they missed out,' she conceded lightly. 'Unless you really do spend all your time making indecent amounts of money and attending film premières.' Not alone, but she felt strangely reluctant to bring his glittering companions into the conversation.

'I like to think my life is more balanced than that.' His female family members might have disputed this. Actually, they frequently did. 'What do you want to know? Ask away.'

It amused him that his passenger didn't appear to appreciate what an extraordinary invitation this was. He still didn't know what impulse had made him extend it. Volunteering information was not something he usually did. After a couple of incidents when he had first found himself in the media spotlight Antonio had turned being guarded and discreet into an art form, much to the intense frustration of those who pursued him.

'Seriously.'

He shrugged and said, 'Why not?' His theory was that while he kept her angry or interested she wasn't stressing about her imminent visit to the hospital.

'Well, knowing your views on making lifelong commitments when you're young, as I now do, and thanks for sharing that with me,' she said with deep sincerity, 'I was wondering how old you were when Tamara was born.'

His head turned and for a brief moment their eyes met. She saw the acknowledgment of her hit reflected in his face. Fleur settled back in her seat, satisfied she had made her point.

'I'm not totally sure,' he said a moment later.

Her eyes widened. 'Not sure? The birth of their child is not the sort of thing that most people forget.'

Under the flickering street lamps Fleur saw an expression she couldn't pin down flicker across his lean face. 'I wasn't around at the time.'

'So you weren't there at the birth.' Her heart went out to the mother giving birth alone.

'Tamara's mother and I were not together when she was born.'

'But Tamara lives with you now…?'

'Her mother died a short time ago.'

'I'm sorry.' It seemed inadequate, but what else could she say that wasn't equally trite?

'Thank you, but Miranda has not been part of my life for many years. But, yes, when she's not running away, Tamara is now living with me. It is a…*new* arrangement.'

'I suppose it can be hard for fathers when their little girls start to grow up,' she conceded generously.

'This situation is different.'

Fleur shrugged. 'I suppose we all think something is different when it happens to us.'

His vocal cords chose that moment to start acting independently of his brain and Antonio heard himself tell a total stranger, 'I only met my daughter a week ago.'

Fleur's first thought was that she had misheard him. 'A week…?'

'Eight days, to be precise.' By all means be precise, Antonio, while you strip your soul bare to satisfy her curiosity.

Antonio's father had been a man who held some pretty inflexible beliefs when it came to manly behaviour. High on the list of things that were signs of weakness and never to be indulged in by *real* men were crying, whining and talking about your feelings.

If Antonio had displayed any of these undesirable traits as a child his father had been disappointed…he had looked at his son and shaken his head.

For Antonio, who had worshipped his father, a sound beating would have been infinitely preferable to that shake of the head.

Even allowing for the balancing strong female influence in his life, something of his father's attitude had inevitably coloured his own behaviour. As an adult it never occurred to him to seek out a shoulder, not even a pretty one, to cry on when the going got tough. And he most certainly did not blurt out private and personal details to total strangers.

Until now.

'You didn't have any contact with her while she was growing up?'

He could hear the frost in her voice. 'None at all.' He'd already told this woman far too much; he wasn't about to defend himself to her.

Lips compressed, Fleur turned her head and looked out the window. She didn't know why she felt disappointed. It wasn't as if the things she had read about him suggested he was big on family values. He was a selfish, hedonistic egotist and they didn't generally make the best fathers in the world.

'And you're surprised she ran away?' He ignored the child all her life and then on a whim decided he wanted to play at being father. What did he expect? she thought scornfully, turning back to look at him.

'So you blame me? You think tonight was my fault?'

'It's really none of my business.'

'Well, that hasn't stopped you from expressing an opinion so far.'

The angry words burst from Fleur. 'Well, I just think—' She stopped and bit her lip. 'Well, there's more to being a father than DNA. It's a title you have to earn—' She stopped again and turned her head to the window. 'Sorry, it's not my business…I just think…I'm sure you don't give a damn what I think…why would you?'

Why do I? He thought about the lies that had been printed about him, and his indifference to them, and asked himself again…why did he care about the opinion of an inquisitive female he had never set eyes an until today?

'You sit there looking so smug and superior, thinking—'

'You don't know what I'm thinking,' she protested.

'You don't think so? Try this!' All the anger and frustration he had been feeling for the past week was in his eyes as without warning he pulled the car to the side of the road, brought it to a halt on the grass verge and switched off the engine.

It was a stretch of road without lights and they were immediately plunged into darkness. Fleur instinctively shrank back in her seat, her eyes widening as she heard the clasp of his belt click. He switched off the car headlights and they were immediately plunged into total inky blackness.

It was the sort of darkness that had texture.

Fleur shivered. Her eyes were wide, straining in the darkness. She couldn't see him, but she could hear the sound of him breathing and feel his anger vibrating in the enclosed space.

The sound of his voice made her start.

'You think that I'm a selfish absentee father who has just decided to play at families.'

As this was almost exactly what she was thinking Fleur remained silent. It didn't seem wise to aggravate farther someone who, for all she knew, could be a dangerous maniac on his days off.

One thing she did know was that he definitely *wasn't* the ice-cool character portrayed in those glossy magazines. She had begun to wonder if the authors of those pieces had ever even met him. If they had they could not possibly have missed the combustible quality that lay there just beneath the surface. She had been all too aware of it from the moment she had laid eyes on him.

Her stomach churned sickly with apprehension as she waited for him to speak.

'That is a very eloquent silence.'

Her eyes had begun to adapt to the lack of light and she could make out his outline. It was large and threatening. 'You're scaring me.'

The silence that followed her breathy confession was heavy and oppressive. Then to her relief he clicked a switch and the interior of the plush car was filled with weak light.

A gusty sigh escaped her tight, aching throat.

He dragged a hand through his dark hair and looked at her pale face. 'You scare easily.'

It might not be his fault that the pale light drew attention to the hard, chiselled angles of his face, making him look sinister and dangerous, but it was his fault that he had scared her witless.

'No, I don't,' she retorted with feeling.

A grimace that might have suggested regret crossed his face. 'I'm sorry,' he said, pressing his head deep into the leather head rest.

Sorry was a word she suspected didn't cross his lips too frequently. She watched as he stared out the window. The thoughts he appeared lost in were, if his expression was any measure, pretty dark. 'I didn't know of her existence until now.'

'Whose existence?'

A muscle alongside his mouth clenched as his head turned. His blue eyes found hers. 'Tamara's.'

Fleur grimaced in concentration and wrinkled her nose as she tried to follow what he was saying. 'How could you not know you had a daughter?'

'I did not know until last week that there was a Tamara. I didn't know that Miranda was pregnant. My daughter and I are total strangers.'

He watched her almond-shaped eyes fly open and cursed under his breath. What was it about her, he wondered, that loosened his tongue?

'Strangers?' she echoed.

He nodded, reliving as he did so the moment he had been given the first glimpse of his daughter as she'd climbed out of the back seat of the Bentley. His trademark objectivity had been history.

She's mine…

Fatherhood might be more than some matching strands of DNA, but in that moment what Antonio had felt had been nothing less than a connection.

However, whatever hope he might have held that Tamara also felt that connection had been quickly dashed. Not content with abandoning Tamara, her so-called father, Charles Finch, had obviously done a number on her. And Antonio was clearly the villain of the piece, the heartless man who was stealing her away from the only home she had ever known and a father who, or so he'd told her, would give anything to keep her. And so his daughter never looked at him with anything but hate in her eyes.

'That's…that's…'

The past faded as beside him and very much in the present Fleur shook her head slowly from side to side.

'That's what she meant when she said you weren't her real father?'

He nodded.

'Her father—the other one, I mean—does she have…? Is he…?'

'He's alive.' His expression was savage as he tacked a furious volley of Spanish onto the terse statement.

Fleur didn't understand a word, but she was guessing—it didn't seem a big leap—he wasn't expressing warm affection for the other man.

'I suppose,' she conceded, 'under the circumstances you're bound to resent him, but you can't really blame the poor man, can you? I mean, I don't know the circumstances—'

'No, you don't.'

'But this must be a tough situation for him too.'

'Yes, the *poor* man has suffered so much, but you know what they say about karma—what goes around comes around. We can only hope that he will get all he deserves one day.' And Antonio really hoped that he would be around to see it…better still deliver it!

Puzzled by the edge to his voice that didn't match the sentiment of his words, she studied him uncertainly.

His lips curled into a sardonic smile. 'You are trying to get into my head again, aren't you, *querida*?'

The husky accusation brought a guilty flush to her cheeks. 'I've told you, it's not somewhere I've any desire to be,' she told him primly.

'Maybe you just can't help yourself where I'm concerned?' he suggested silkily.

Now that was a really scary thought. 'And maybe *you're* totally deluded—' She broke off, her eyes widening as without warning he leaned across and took her face between his big hands.

'What do you think you're doing?' She felt the warmth of his breath on her cheek and with a whimper closed her eyes tight shut.

'It is your birthday,' he said in a voice that seemed much more thickly accented than she had noticed before.

'I know that.'

He tilted her framed face up to him. If he didn't kiss that mouth he would always wonder… 'Is it not almost obligatory to kiss a person on her birthday?'

'Not this per…' She sucked in a deep startled breath and stilled as she felt the feathery touch of his lips on first one eyelid, then the other. At the corner of her mouth his touch was equally light.

This was fine. This she could cope with, even laugh about with Jane at a later date. *The day Fleur got kissed by a Spanish billionaire* would be a joke between them.

All I have to do, she told herself, is not make a big thing of it and breathe…yes, breathing was important.

His head lifted.

'Right, I consider myself kissed. Can we get on?'

'Kissed…?' he echoed, his blue eyes glittering with amusement and a lot of other things that she didn't want to put a name to. 'You haven't been kissed, *querida*,' he drawled.

Then before she had a chance to react he lowered his mouth to hers.

His warm lips moved against her mouth. She tried to signal her disapproval by not reacting, but there was a raw hunger in the skilful, sensuous friction that she couldn't resist.

Didn't want to resist.

His mouth lifted fractionally and Fleur gave a fractured moan before he claimed her parted lips again. This time the hunger he had leashed slipped a notch.

As if he had all the time in the world Antonio slid his tongue deep into the warm, intimate crevices of her mouth. Tasting her and letting her taste him.

As bright lights exploded behind her closed eyelids Fleur moaned into his mouth and kissed him back, winding her arms around his neck, her fingers trailing in the dark strands that curled at his nape.

He said something indistinct against her mouth and lifted his mouth. Leaning back into his seat, he sat there staring straight ahead and breathing hard.

At some point between him unwinding her hands from around his neck and fastening his seat belt her brain started functioning again.

Well, I suppose that now I *have* been kissed.

She lifted a shaky hand to her tender lips and swallowed past the constriction in her aching throat. Oh, yes, there was no doubt about it—she had been kissed!

And what a kiss.

Antonio turned the key in the ignition, nothing in his manner suggesting that he had just kissed her until she forgot her own name. And he still hadn't said a word.

Resentment mingled with the cocktail of confusion, shame and excitement that was already swirling in Fleur's veins as she watched him.

As if it had never happened!

Kissing me probably registered somewhere below combing his hair on his scale of the totally forgettable, she decided wrathfully.

And I, stupid idiot that I am, will be left comparing every kiss I ever receive with that one.

Before releasing the handbrake he swivelled his glance her way. 'Happy Birthday.'

For a brief moment their eyes clung. The searing heat in his sent a shocking rush of heat through Fleur's body. Knowing that he hadn't wanted that kiss to stop any more than she had was not the salve to her pride she had imagined it would be.

Being the victim of a helpless passion was one thing. It was frustrating, sure, and horribly embarrassing, but it was safe. Knowing that the object of her desire for some inexplicable reason wanted her right back...now that scared her witless!

About a quarter of a mile down the road they hit the outskirts of the town and almost immediately the hospital came into view.

If anyone had told her yesterday that she would be weak with relief to see a hospital Fleur would have laughed in their face. Yesterday, she thought, flashing a look of seething dislike at the man beside her, she had not met Antonio Rochas.

CHAPTER SEVEN

FLEUR sat in an alcove off the waiting room feeling invisible. They had told her that the painkillers the doctor had insisted on prescribing would be up from the pharmacy directly. She glanced at the clock on the wall and saw she had been there for almost thirty minutes. Maybe they were taking the scenic route.

She looked around at the steady stream of humanity bustling past her all with a purpose, but none of their purposes involved helping her get out of here. Had they forgotten she was there?

Almost immediately she felt guilty for being so impatient. It wasn't that she resented having to wait her turn, and the treatment she had received had been excellent, it was just the place made her want to crawl out of her skin.

Somehow she couldn't imagine anyone forgetting Antonio Rochas was here. Her brow furrowed as she gave an exasperated sigh. For someone who had decided that she was going to blank him, his convoluted family problems and his wretched kiss from her mind totally, she had been thinking about him a lot.

Still, at least it stopped her thinking about the hospital smell. She picked up a newspaper someone had left on the seat beside her and began to skim through the pages, although she wasn't actually able to concentrate on the stories.

The elderly woman opposite waved her stick to get Fleur's attention. 'What does my horoscope say, dear?'

Fleur smiled and turned to the appropriate page. 'What star sign are you?'

'Virgo.'

'Me too,' Fleur said. 'Let's see,' she said, stabbing the appropriate column with a finger. 'It says here that "an unexpected meeting will have life-changing consequences."' She stopped reading and heaved a sigh. Even the stars were conspiring against her, it would seem! Not that she believed that sort of stuff. A person made their own destiny irrespective of whether Jupiter was rising in Capricorn or whatever. All the same, that was spooky. 'I don't have my reading glasses with me—would you like the paper?'

At this rate, next I'll be seeing him in the tea leaves!

The grey-haired figure smiled her gratitude as Fleur limped across. 'So young to have problems with your eyesight,' she said, accepting the folded newspaper.

'It runs in the family,' Fleur improvised shamelessly.

'And such pretty eyes too.'

Did Antonio think her eyes were pretty?

'Stop that, Fleur!' she told herself severely.

'Pardon, dear?' the old lady said.

Fleur shook her head and limped back to her place and, with nothing much else to do, her thoughts drifted. Inevitably they drifted in the direction of a tall dark Spaniard. She had no doubt that the fact she had walked, or rather limped, into the place at his side had a lot to do with her being attended to so swiftly.

Just as she was considering the shallowness in human nature that made people respond to a famous face that way the nurse who had attended to her while her leg was sutured walked past.

'Still here?' she said looking sympathetic.

Fleur nodded.

'I was wondering,' she began tentatively, 'do you know how Tamara Rochas...' She stopped and gave a rueful grimace. 'Sorry, I expect you can't discuss patients with non-relatives.' And as a completely disinterested party I ought not to be asking.

'Well, you're not exactly a stranger, are you?' The girl smiled.

Fleur, not quite sure how to respond, shrugged and said cautiously, 'Not exactly.'

'If you like,' offered the cheerful nurse, 'I'll show you to her room. It's on my way to the canteen.'

'I'm supposed to wait here for my painkillers,' Fleur said, thinking, This is not something I should even be considering.

'And wait you will. The computers were down for two hours this morning and they're still catching up on the backlog. And to make matters worse Pharmacy has half its staff off with the flu thing. It'll probably take them another half-hour at least to get your prescription sorted.'

Having been part, albeit an incidental part, of the rescue it would be nice to see for herself that the victim was all right.

Rationalisation, said the snide voice in her head.

Fleur tilted her chin and said, 'You're really kind.' If Antonio was there...well, that had nothing whatever to do with her decision.

'Family friend, are you?' the inquisitive nurse asked as she pressed the lift button for the third floor.

The query brought home to Fleur just how inappropriate her actions were. She might know a little more concerning the details of Antonios' Rochas's strained relationship with his daughter, but the bottom line was she was a stranger.

A stranger the patient's father had kissed.

Fleur chose her words with care, extremely aware that this

was the perfect opportunity to smother any foolish rumours before they started circulating.

'Just a neighbour. I hardly know him.' What, she wondered, would be the consequences if she were to claim a closer relationship? Mention the fact that her lips were still tingling from his kiss.

'Sure you are.'

Fleur didn't respond to the girl's conspiratorial wink.

'No, *really*,' she said firmly.

The nurse's face dropped. 'Really? We thought maybe you and he were…?'

Fleur adopted a droll expression. 'Yes, that's *really* likely, isn't it?'

The girl's glance slid over Fleur in her borrowed clothes. 'We can dream, can't we?' The other girl sighed.

Feeling rather deflated that it had been so depressingly easy to convince the nurse that the notion of her and Antonio being an item was ludicrous, she leaned against the wall of the lift and thought, Dream about being Antonio's lover? Not a good idea.

'Fifth door on the left—3B,' supplied her guide with a smile before the lift door closed.

Fleur counted the doors off and then knocked twice. When there was no response, she tentatively pushed the door open and found herself inside a small hallway.

Fleur was relieved the nurses' station to her left was unoccupied. The moment she opened the door she had realised that this was not a good idea. The man was going to think she was stalking him.

And I'm not…?

She hesitated a fatal moment too long. If she hadn't she would not have heard the voices. One was high and young, one deep. One more backwards step and she'd have been free.

You still are free, she told herself.

So why then was she walking towards that voice as though someone had tugged the other end of a string and was reeling her in?

Of the four rooms that opened off the area, two appeared unoccupied. One door was open.

From where she stood to one side of the doorway she could see the hospital bed, but its occupant could not see her. As she hesitated a tall figure who had been out of view came to stand beside the bed. He put his hands flat on the edge and bent towards the figure who held an oxygen mask in her hand.

'You should not upset yourself.' Antonio took the mask from her fingers and placed it to her face.

His daughter looked almost as pale as the pillows she was propped up against.

Tamara snatched the mask away. 'Don't try and pretend you care about me, or that my mother meant anything to you,' she sneered. 'What was she—a one-night stand?'

'I do not do one-night stands.'

Antonio was conscious that he had made the same angry assertion only a couple of weeks earlier. On that occasion it had been in response to his sister's taunt that he was in no position to discuss relationships because he'd never had one, only a series of one-night stands.

His angry disclaimer had cut no ice with Sophia. He was used to his volatile sister's cutting ripostes, but this one had stuck in his mind.

'Your one-night stands may last six months, a year, even, but, believe me, Antonio, they're not relationships. A relationship requires that you give something of yourself and you don't even know how.'

'So did you love her?'

There was a silence.

Antonio watched Tamara's thin frame stiffen as though anticipating a blow.

An image formed in Antonio's head: flawless skin, full lips painted red, and eyes that could radiate an innocence their owner had not possessed. It was a lovely face. A face inextricably linked with deceit and humiliation. The deceit had been hers, the humiliation his. And when you were nineteen and in love humiliation could be pretty devastating.

Falling in love with Miranda had been a life-shaping experience for Antonio. She had taught him an important lesson. You could allow your passions to rule you or you could rule them.

Antonio had made his choice.

Where his emotions were concerned he had taught himself to step back, to be objective. Having the women in his life complain that he gave nothing of himself seemed infinitely preferable to Antonio than the alternative.

But there was now a female in his life whom he could not step back from—one he could not be objective about.

He knew exactly what he had to say.

'I was very much in love with your mother.'

The girl studied his face suspiciously. *'You were...?'*

'I was, and I can honestly say I have never loved a woman since.' Loving required trust and Antonio had no intention of trusting a woman again.

For no reason at all he found himself thinking about Fleur, those big, innocent eyes, and he felt tender feelings stir.

Then he thought about her mouth and was instantly locked into a steamy fantasy.

It was only when an attractive nurse in a crisp white uniform bustled in and said something he didn't hear that Antonio managed to drag his thoughts away from the erotic images dancing in his mind.

* * *

Fleur hadn't stuck around to see how the girl responded to his confession.

As she limped down the corridor her emotions were in turmoil. Antonio the man with the playboy reputation, she could deal with…*sort of.* Antonio the man who had only ever loved one woman, and lost her…now that was a very different prospect.

She hated this shift of feelings that was taking place inside her. But then maybe, she mused darkly, she was only getting what she deserved. Eavesdropping was a contemptible thing.

She had decided to despise Antonio Rochas before she'd even met him. Now she was presented with the possibility that underneath the cynicism and macho posturing there was a man capable of deep feeling. A one-woman man…

Did he compare all women with the one he had lost…?

Had he been thinking about his tragic lost love when he'd kissed her? Then, recalling the glazed heat in his glittering eyes, she decided not. It seemed unlikely that his brain had been involved at all during that brief passionate exchange!

And as her own brain had flat-lined the moment he had touched her, Fleur didn't feel she was in a position to sneer.

Two nurses were emerging from the room next door when Fleur limped past, they looked startled to see her. Fleur just smiled and tried to look as though she were somewhere she was meant to be, which undoubtedly she wasn't.

The helpful nurse had been wrong. She didn't have to wait thirty minutes—it was nearly an hour before she received her painkillers. With time on her hands her imagination went into overdrive.

Had they argued over something trivial? Had both been too proud and stubborn to be the first one to say they were wrong?

She supposed that she was never going to know the real story.

* * *

Antonio stayed for a while after Tamara had fallen asleep. Sometimes she seemed so adult, but in repose, the defiance and belligerence absent from her face, his daughter looked like the child she actually was.

Her vulnerability touched him, aroused a fierce protectiveness in him.

Was this the way fathers felt? He wouldn't know because the blonde had been right—there was more to fatherhood than matching DNA.

It suddenly hit him all the things he had missed. What had she been like as a baby, a toddler…? He would never know. The sense of loss hit him with a force so strong that it felt like a blade sliding between his ribs.

He felt a volatile mixture of emotions as he looked at this child who was a part of him. He suddenly realised the enormity of having the responsibility for another life. He found himself admiring single parents who raised their children alone.

Fleur had made it through the glass turnstile exit of Casualty when she saw Antonio.

He looked so alone.

He was standing, his hands dug deep in his pockets, his back set to the wind. He wasn't looking in her direction and even if he had been she wasn't sure he would have noticed her. His expression in profile suggested he was a man with a lot on his mind. *Vulnerable*…mentally she deleted the word that flashed into her head.

Do not even *think* about feeling sorry for him, she lectured herself sternly. If ever there was a man who could look after himself, it was Antonio Rochas.

Just walk past, Fleur…walk past and keep walking.

It was sound advice.

She nearly made it, very nearly. She had almost readied the

rank of taxis when her conscience proved stronger than her instincts for self-preservation.

'You're an idiot, Fleur,' she muttered to herself as she hurried back up the rain-slick path.

She stopped just a little out of his line of vision and studied him, trying to figure out what it was, beside the obvious, which made her react to him differently from the way she ever had to any other man.

It defied logic.

'You're still here…?'

Antonio turned his head and levered his broad shoulders from the wall. 'I came out here for some fresh air while I waited.'

'For what?'

'You.'

'Why?'

'When I arrive with a lady I like to see that she gets safely to her destination.'

'How sweet and gallant.' She lifted her eyes to his and sketched a smile. 'Though less sweet and gallant when you take into account your bed is usually her destination. So I suppose you have a vested interest in making sure she gets there.'

Antonio released a startled hissing gasp through his clenched teeth. Then to her dismay grinned. His blue eyes danced with mockery as he asked, 'Is that where you are expecting to end up…?'

Wondering when she was going to stop blurting out the first thing that came into her head, Fleur willed her fiery cheeks to stop burning.

'I would prefer to spend the night in this place—' she tipped her head in the direction of the big building behind them '—and you know how much I love hospitals.'

Antonio didn't dispute her angry claim. 'They tell me they

are letting you go home?' His grin faded as his glance dropped to her leg.

She nodded, relieved that he had dropped the subject of his bed, then stiffened. '*They* should not have been telling you anything.'

Irritatingly her annoyance seemed to amuse him. 'I promise they did not reveal any medical details. I don't even know if you had stitches?'

'Yes,' she admitted. 'And a tetanus shot. You were right.'

'I usually am.'

'Infallible and modest.' He would have been even smugger if he had heard the doctor tell her that a fraction deeper and a tendon would have been severed.

Her comment drew a grin from him, this time it seemed more tired than sardonic.

'Do you have to come back to the clinic?'

'No, they topped up my tetanus cover and gave me an antibiotic jab.' She shook the paper bag in her hand. 'Painkillers.' Which she did need; now the local had worn off her leg was aching with a vengeance. 'And I can go back to my GP to have them taken out. So I'm sorted. How's Tamara?'

Antonio visibly tensed at the name. 'They're keeping her in overnight,' he said abruptly.

'But she's…'

'They say she'll be fine, but—' his eyes swept across her upturned features and a disturbing expression slid into his eyes '—you already know that, don't you?'

Fleur stiffened and looked up at him warily through her lashes. '*I do…?*' Overplaying the innocence big time, mocked the voice in her head.

'The nurses mentioned our visitor,' Antonio revealed, stretching one arm above his head and rotating first one shoulder and then the other to relieve the knots of tension in his spine and shoulders.

A distracted expression slid across Fleur's face as she imagined the things going on under his shirt… Things like taut muscle rippling beneath satiny golden skin. A hoarse sound escaped her throat as she lowered her eyes and grunted. 'Why do you automatically assume that was me?'

'The interesting limp, blond hair and golden eyes were clues,' he revealed drily.

Her eyes flew upwards. 'They did not notice what colour my eyes were!' she scoffed.

'No, but I did.'

His eyes locked onto hers and as she registered the explicitly sensual gleam Fleur's stomach took a diving lurch. 'I thought I'd look in,' she admitted, tugging at the neckline of her borrowed top.

One dark eyebrow lifted. 'But changed your mind?'

'I got as far as the door, but…'

'You saw me,' he inserted drily. 'Were you worried I would kiss you again?'

Hoped. The colour in her cheeks perceptibly heightened. Fleur shrugged while fighting to contain her growing panic. 'Not really. I thought I was quite safe from your unwanted attentions in front of your daughter.'

'Unwanted…?'

She squared her jaw. 'You think I enjoy being mauled by strange men?'

'I can't speak in general, but if we're talking specifics—'

Fleur, who didn't want to talk specifically or any other way about that kiss in the car, cut across him with a high-pitched, 'I just didn't want to intrude.'

The muscles around his mouth quivered as his lips compressed into a hard line. 'An intrusion might have been welcome.'

'Well, it's good that there was no real harm.' At least not to Tamara. Fleur was less sure that she could claim the same, and she wasn't thinking about her leg! 'Are you staying here tonight?'

'They said there's not much point—they gave her something to help her sleep—but I will anyway,' he said, flexing his shoulders once more before shoving his hands back into his pockets.

'Then you couldn't take me home, could you?' she pointed out. 'Unless your talents include the ability to be in two places at once.'

'The idea was I take you home and then come back.'

Get in a car with him again... It would be like an alcoholic getting a job in a distillery! Accepting you have a problem is the first step, Fleur, she told herself. And, oh, boy, do I have a problem!

'There's absolutely no need, and anyway you wouldn't want to risk Tamara waking up and you not being there.'

'I seriously doubt if seeing my face when she wakes up would speed her recovery. But then you already know that too, don't you? You'll have such a lot to tell your friends.'

'I'm not a gossip and I didn't ask to be a witness to your private family arguments,' she reminded him, stung by the suggestion she couldn't wait to rush out to share his secrets with the world. Why exactly had he shared them with her? 'And, frankly, I've got enough problems of my own without sharing yours.'

'You didn't ask to be kissed either, but you enjoyed that.' His eyes skimmed over her face and his voice dropped a husky octave as he added a husky, 'So did I.' His long lashes swept upwards from the angle of his chiselled cheekbones as his blue eyes meshed with hers.

'You sound surprised,' she observed huskily.

His brows lifted as he looked struck by her remark. 'I suppose I was,' he admitted.

'Because I look like someone who doesn't know how to kiss.'

This spiky comment drew a laugh from Antonio. The un-inhibited and extremely attractive sound made several people look curiously in their direction. It made Fleur's hopelessly receptive stomach muscles quiver frantically.

'With that mouth…' The last traces of laughter faded from his face as his glance came to rest on the lush outline. 'You could not fail to be a good kisser. That mouth,' he said, staring at it hard, 'was made for kissing.'

Not surprisingly Fleur, who was standing there with her feet nailed to the floor with dark waves of sheer longing lapping around her ankles, couldn't think of a suitably glib retort.

The perplexed pucker that pleated his forehead deepened. 'No, it was my reaction that surprised me,' he admitted, still staring at her mouth.

I really wish he wouldn't.

'The last time I made love in a car I was in my teens.'

'Knowledge I could have lived without.' But not for the reason her caustic tone suggested.

In her head she could see female hands sliding under his shirt and along the smooth golden skin of his strong, supple back just the way she had wanted her to.

'Around you my control is…not good,' he revealed with admirable understatement. Around her he had less control than a kid deluged by the first rush of male hormones.

'And we did *not* make love!' That had only happened in her head and, though her mind was pretty messed up, she could still differentiate between what was real and what was a figment of her feverish imagination. *Just!*

'That had very little to do with good judgement. If that car hadn't sounded its horn…'

'What car?' she said without thinking.

Antonio tilted his dark head fractionally, as if acknowledging a compliment. 'I'm flattered.'

And so pleased with himself that she wanted to kick him. 'Oh, that car…'

'Yes, that car.'

His indulgent tone set her teeth on edge. 'Right, well, I should be getting home. I have to pick up Sandy.'

'Don't bother. I'll drop him over in the morning.'

'There's no need.'

'I want to.'

His tone was far more forceful and emphatic than the subject warranted. Now if he'd been saying, I want *you*…

Trying to act as if she weren't shaking feverishly and her body hadn't been engulfed by a flash of heat, Fleur gave a shrug that suggested she didn't care one way or the other and began to walk away.

She had gone a few yards when she looked back over her shoulder. 'You're really not that good a kisser, you know.'

'You are.'

If he'd smiled it would have passed as a joke, but he didn't smile.

Hunching her shoulders, Fleur almost ran down the path, oblivious to the pain in her leg. Clearly he was a man who had to have the last word… The alternative was, well, actually, the alternative was plain ridiculous.

CHAPTER EIGHT

FLEUR dumped the bowl of blackberries she had just picked from the hedge on the drainer and, pausing only to kick off her Wellingtons, hurried to answer the door.

Smoothing down her hair, she opened the door. 'Sorry, I was in the garden…' She stopped, her eyes widening as she identified her visitor. 'Hello…Tamara, isn't it?'

Two days after the near-death lake drama and not wet or nearly dead the youngster was revealed as tall and slender with the makings of real beauty in the stunning bones of her softly youthful face and big liquid brown fawn-like eyes.

Just as Fleur had predicted, in a couple of years when those awkward coltish angles softened and the curves filled out Antonio was going to have a whole new set of problems, she reflected, unable to repress an uncharitable smile at the thought.

'*He* said I had to come and thank you…' Looking resentful as only a teenager could, she gestured towards the lane.

Fleur registered the Range Rover, then the outline of a figure in the driver's seat, and tensed.

'Like I wasn't going to say thank you anyway,' the girl added with a sarcastic sniff. '*He* didn't have to tell me to.'

'Would you like to come in?' Fleur asked, knowing when not to offer an opinion. It wasn't as though Antonio would thank her for speaking up for him. Antonio who had sent his daughter but not come himself. She would be well within her rights to march up to that car and demand the explanation she deserved!

She didn't, because that would make him think she gave a damn whether or not he kept his promises.

Her glance flickered covertly towards the parked vehicle. For someone, she mused, who apparently put such great store by good manners, his could do with some work!

Was he sitting out there because he was afraid that she would want to take up where they had left off, which, now she came to think about it, was nowhere. Whatever the reason, he needn't have worried—she had received the message loud and clear when one of the female gardeners had brought Sandy back the next morning.

Fleur had had no problem translating, 'To save you the bother of calling for him,' as, 'You've got no excuse to come calling at the big house now.' It was clear to her that he considered that kiss a massive lapse of judgement and not a lapse he felt inclined to repeat in the cold light of day.

And neither did she.

Tamara looked curiously past Fleur into the cottage, but shook her head. 'I'd better not. *He's* in a hurry.'

'Some other time, maybe, and I'm glad you're feeling better,' Fleur said.

'Thanks to you.' The words were minus the sulky tones that had laced the conversation to this point.

'You're welcome,' Fleur replied cheerfully. 'But I didn't actually have much to do with saving you,' she admitted.

The girl frowned and in the process looked remarkably like a softer version of her father. 'But...'

'That was your father,' Fleur inserted. 'But then I'm sure you already know that.' The girl's expressive face was a fair indication that she knew nothing of the sort, but, pretending not to notice, Fleur added, 'When he dived down for that last time…' She closed her eyes, a shudder running through her body as without warning she was back there staring at the still water…waiting and praying.

'I really thought he wasn't coming back up…' She didn't have to pretend the husky emotion in her voice as her thoughts returned to that awful moment.

Then exhaling a gusty sigh and rubbing her arms, which were covered in a rash of goose-flesh, she lifted her eyes. The astonishment chasing across the youthful features of Antonio's daughter was almost comical. Clearly this was the first time the girl had realised that the man she claimed to loathe had risked his life for her.

'Well, he wasn't, was he? Coming back up, that is—not without you, at any rate.'

Tamara stared at Fleur. 'But he doesn't even want me.'

'Then he has a funny way of showing it.'

'It's only a matter of time before he sends me back.' Fleur could hear the flicker of uncertainty mingled with despair in the young voice.

Her own expression was sympathetic as she suggested, 'And you think acting like the teenager from hell will speed up the process? Have you thought about being nice, talking to him, telling him how unhappy you are?'

The girl's brows knit in a frown as she insisted, 'He doesn't care about me.'

'Has he said that?'

'He doesn't have to. It's *obvious*,' the youngster retorted defensively. 'It would have solved his problem if I'd drowned.'

Fleur watched her eyes fill with tears and told herself that the smart thing to do would be to say nothing. Getting involved with the Rochas family was the last thing she wanted to do. She would get no thanks and if anything went wrong—a more-than-likely scenario—she'd be the first person he'd blame.

'And I suppose you told him that.' So much for not getting involved, Fleur.

The girl lifted her chin defiantly and shrugged. 'He didn't deny it.'

As bad as her father, Fleur thought, stifling a sigh as she studied the stubborn set of the girl's jaw. 'Well, he wouldn't, would he? Not when he's got that whole macho, man-of-steel-never-explain-yourself-to-anyone thing going on.'

The waspishly exasperated retort drew a reluctant chuckle from the girl. Pausing halfway up the path and unashamedly eavesdropping, Antonio paused. It was the first time he had heard his daughter laugh.

'Don't you like him?'

Fleur, surprised by the question, considered it.

'Your father isn't the sort of person that people like.' Like was a tepid term and *nothing* about Antonio was tepid. She thought about his mouth and the way her insides dissolved when she looked at it and said, 'He's the sort of person people love or loathe.'

'Which camp do you fall into, Fleur?'

The colour flew darkly to Fleur's cheeks as a tall figure moved from the concealing shadow of a holly bush. He was wearing a grey cashmere sweater, dark, well-tailored casual trousers and a natural air of authority. He looked drop-dead gorgeous. So no change there.

Damn the man, he was always where you didn't want him to be. He was always making you feel things you didn't want to feel, she thought with a gulp of sheer despair as she realised that she had no control whatever over her reaction to him.

She had managed to go twenty-five years without feeling primitive sexual awareness so why now? Why him?

One dark brow at a satirical slant, his blue eyes shone with malicious humour as he scanned Fleur's feverishly flushed face. 'Or should I not ask?'

'You're an expert at doing things you shouldn't,' she retorted, then almost immediately wished she hadn't, because the comment brought his gaze to her mouth and she knew he was thinking about that kiss.

Worse still, so was she!

'How long have you been standing there?' she demanded, lifting her chin.

'How do you think I feel?' his daughter appealed to Fleur. 'He never lets me out of his sight, and he won't let me see my real dad.'

Fleur turned shocked eyes on Antonio. 'I'm sure that's not true.'

The girl laughed bitterly. 'You think that because you don't know him like I do,' she claimed.

A very timely reminder, thought Fleur. You don't know him at all, which made the fact that when he was this close she could think about nothing else but how his body would feel against her own all the more hideously appalling!

'For the moment it's better if you settle into your new life.'

The teenager glanced over at Fleur. 'See…I told you so.' Then, whipping her head back to her father, she snapped, 'I don't want a new life; I liked my old life.'

'You'll adapt,' Antonio told her grimly. 'How is your leg?' he said, turning to Fleur.

'It's fine. I get the stitches out Thursday.'

'But it could have been otherwise. Something you might like to remember, Tamara, the next time you feel the urge to demonstrate your independence. It is very often innocent by-standers who get hurt.'

The girl flushed and looked guiltily towards Fleur. 'It wasn't my fault.'

'One of the first lessons you need to learn, Tamara, is that a person, at least one with any guts, takes responsibility for the consequences of their actions and doesn't try and blame someone else.'

Fleur wasn't surprised to see the tears spring to the youngster's eyes. The average hard-bitten board member of a multi-national, she reflected, would have struggled not to be intimidated by his coldly peremptory tone and icy manner.

'Go wait for me in the car, Tamara,' he added tiredly as he switched his attention back to Fleur, who wished he hadn't. The dark shadows under his eyes ought to have made him look haggard, but actually they made him look even more darkly dangerous in a sexy way.

'I wi—'

Fleur breathed again as his attention switched back to his daughter.

'You will do as I ask for once and try not to inform every passer-by that you are being kidnapped.'

With one final resentful look at his stern profile, the girl flounced off.

Fleur could not control her exasperation. 'You're such a prat!'

His dark head came around with a snap.

Refusing to back down in the face of the astonished hauteur stamped on his autocratic features, she pursed her lips and added firmly, 'Don't look at me like that; you are. A grade-A, total and absolute…' She heaved a sigh and shook her head. 'I'm wasting my breath, aren't I?'

Some of the frostiness faded from his dark features as he gave an expressive shrug. 'I am willing to admit I have flaws.'

She closed her eyes for a split second and thought, No visible ones.

Fleur pushed aside an image of him naked—drawn from her imagination—and, opening her eyes, released a rueful, though not totally convincing, laugh.

'My, what a concession,' she retorted huskily.

'And no experience in being a father.'

She tried very hard *not* to see the flicker of pain, quickly concealed, that flashed briefly in his eyes. She didn't want to feel empathy for this man; it was the short route to emotional complications she could do without.

Fleur's eyes travelled the length of his lean, vital body and she repressed a sigh. Who am I kidding? The man is a walking, breathing complication.

'Well, talking to her would be a start.'

'Madre mía…!' he ejaculated, looking less than grateful for the advice. 'Do you think I have not tried?' He took a deep breath and continued in a more moderate tone. 'It is…*difficult*. The child resents me.'

Fleur looked at him incredulously. 'Is it any wonder?' she asked him. 'You won't let her see the man she's presumably thought of as her father for the past thirteen years. I know your middle name isn't sensitivity, but for goodness' sake!' she breathed, shaking her head in disapproval. 'Surely you must see…'

'I see…yes, I do see.' Sensual lips compressed, he drew a hand across his jaw and glared down at her.

Fleur lifted her brows. 'You see what?'

'I see that your officious, meddlesome behaviour is meant to compensate for the fact you appear to have no life of your own.'

You can almost see the superiority oozing from every pore, she thought, feeling something snap inside as she looked up at him.

'For your information, I *have* a life. I have a great life, which was even greater when you weren't in it.' Frowning and hoping Antonio had not picked up on the unspoken implication that he had somehow become part of her life, Fleur added belligerently, 'And while we're talking about lives, just how great is yours anyhow?

'Oh, I know you make a lot of money and you swan around being seen in the right places with some girl with a surgically enhanced body draped all over you. But I'd say *your* lifestyle is the one that warrents a little scrutiny...' she suggested with a derisive snigger.

'As for meddlesome,' she gritted from between clenched teeth, 'I admit my natural instinct is to pull someone back when they're about to walk off the side of.a cliff.' Breathless but unrepentant for her rant, she stuck out her chin and promised sweetly, 'But in future for you I will make an exception. Actually, if you like I'll point you in the right direction.'

A stunned silence followed her emotional outburst.

It lasted long enough for Fleur to start doubting the wisdom of speaking her mind. Not that she cared if she had offended him or that she didn't believe what she had said was not essentially true, though she supposed that some of his girl-friends' assets might conceivably be natural.

Thinking about some of the more spectacular bodies she'd seen Antonio photographed beside sent her mood into a downward spiral. Attached to those bodies were perfect smiles. Women with those sorts of smiles would routinely tell him how marvellous he was and never, *ever* say something that left the impression they'd quite like to see him jump off a cliff.

'I had no right to make personal comments.'

It was grudging but definitely an admission. Surprised, but trying hard not to show it, Fleur nodded her head warily.

'No, you didn't.'

'You really do come out fighting, don't you...*querida*?'

And he sounded as if he admired the fact... Every time she

thought she had a handle on this man, he did or said something that made her realise he was not always what he seemed.

'Just because you're frustrated doesn't give you the right to take it out on me.'

His heavy eyelids lowered as his bold glance drifted down her body. When he reached her toes he began to work his way up again, really slowly. The action had the result of making Fleur painfully aware of every inch of her body and the way it was reacting to his scrutiny, which was stupid because he was probably compiling a mental list of what was wrong with her.

He got back to her face and it turned out he hadn't been compiling a list of faults.

He fixed her with a gleaming predatory stare that made her sensitive tummy quiver. His voice was a low, throaty purr as he asked, 'Has it occurred to you that *you're* part of the reason I'm frustrated?'

CHAPTER NINE

IT HADN'T, but it was now!

Fleur struggled to maintain at least the illusion of composure as inside she dissolved. Through her lashes she could see the dark colour running along the angles of Antonio's chiselled cheekbones. The glitter in his heavy-lidded eyes drew a fractured sigh from her parted lips.

'I was thinking about the other night when we...'

Fleur shook her head. 'There's nothing you can tell me that I don't already know,' she promised him.

'You have been thinking of it too.' It wasn't a question.

'Not even a little bit.' Sometimes lies were not only justified, they were essential. 'I hate to break it to you, Antonio, but one kiss is really very much like another. You know what your problem is—'

'My kissing technique needs polish?'

Of course, he could sound smug—anyone who kissed like an angel, the fallen variety, could afford to sound so confident. Suddenly Fleur was so mad with him she wanted to hit him. Instead she clenched her hands and tucked them behind her back.

'Your problem is your priorities. We were talking about Tamara. While you carry on preventing her seeing this man she's going to resent you and I for one don't blame her.'

Antonio hissed something that sounded angry under his breath and dragged a hand through the gleaming strands of his dark hair.

Fleur was dismayed to recognise that her reaction to the lessening of screaming sexual tension in the air was ambiguous.

'Do you imagine,' he demanded, rounding on her with a furious scowl, 'that this is a situation of my choosing?'

'Aren't you the one who's just been preaching on about taking responsibility for your own actions?' she countered crossly. 'I think what you've done is positively inhuman.'

'You're a sanctimonious little...' The rest of his sentence was completed in rapid, angry Spanish.

Well, at least he's not thinking about kissing me anymore. Throttling, possibly, she mused, responding to his hostile glare with a smile that visibly raised his aggravation levels.

Antonio took a deep breath and held his hands in front of him, his long fingers extended as he revealed in a flat monotone that obviously masked strong feelings, 'Charles Finch, the man Miranda married before Tamara was born, has made it very clear he does not want to see Tamara. So there it is,' he said, snapping his fingers and pacing restlessly as far as the edge of the paved area.

Fleur, her brow furrowed, watched him walk back. 'I don't understand—?'

A nerve in his strong jaw clenched as he cut across her. 'He wants no contact with Tamara at all. How much clearer can I make it?' His voice grim, he elaborated. 'Finch arrived at my office, told me that Miranda was dead and I had a daughter who was waiting for me in the car. And, before you ask, no, I did *not* misunderstand his motives. No, he was *not* giving us time to get to know one another. I say this because I know that you like to imagine everyone, with the exception of myself, has virtuous motives.'

Fleur blinked and went pale; she just couldn't imagine anyone doing something so…so…*vicious*. *'Seriously…?'*

Though there was absolutely no trace of emotion in Antonio's face, she never doubted that inside he must feel… well, actually, she didn't have a clue. How, she reflected, could you possibly imagine what it would feel like to learn that the love of your life had died and you had fathered a child who was now thirteen in the space of a few minutes?

She had no doubt that Antonio Rochas had nerves of steel and reserves that lesser mortals could only dream of, but coping with all that must have been a big ask even for him!

'Well, it's hardly something I would joke about, is it?'

Fleur felt angry on Tamara's behalf. Antonio might have his faults, but he had to be an improvement on someone like that. 'But that's so cruel—what an awful man!' she exclaimed. 'He doesn't deserve a daughter like Tamara.' She lifted her eyes and saw that Antonio was watching her with a strange expression.

'Do you think I'm an improvement?' he asked.

Fleur thought, You're an improvement on perfect, and flushed. Out loud she admitted gruffly, 'I suppose you have potential.'

His eyes not leaving hers, he inclined his sable head in acknowledgement to her gruff concession.

'Have you told Tamara?'

'What purpose would that serve?' he wanted to know.

'Well, she might not hate you so much.'

Antonio looked at the narrow section of smooth midriff exposed by the skimpy tee shirt she wore and wondered if her skin was as warm and silky as it looked. 'She needs someone to hate and,' he added with a shrug, 'I can take it.'

'Because you're such a tough macho man,' she taunted gently.

'Because I am her father, and I wasn't there when I should

have been. I think that Tamara is a little too fragile…emotionally speaking…for the unvarnished truth just now.'

'So you'll play the bad guy?'

A wolfish grin split his lean face. 'I *am* the bad guy, haven't you heard?' He was surprised to hear himself add, 'Come with us to London for the afternoon.'

'Why?'

Good question. 'The women I know don't need a reason to shop.'

'I'm not the women you know.'

Something moved at the back of his eyes, but before she could put a name to the elusive emotion it was gone and he was smiling, not with his mouth, but with his eyes. It was a disturbing smile that made her already erratic heart rate quicken.

'No, you're not, are you?'

It was hard to decide from his enigmatic tone whether this was a good thing from his point of view or not.

'You want a reason?'

She nodded, thinking that with some things there was no reason. I mean, what reason could there be for her to fall for a man who was only ever going to break her heart?

My God, we don't even live in the same world!

'Well, you've seen us together. You have to admit an umpire would be a good thing.'

'And here was me thinking you liked the idea of my company.'

Her sarcastic smile guttered as his eyes met hers in a long disturbing stare. Tearing her eyes free of the level blue gaze a moment later than she should have left Fleur feeling slightly breathless. Slightly? No, actually a *lot* breathless.

She patted the head of the dog who had wandered sleepily out to see what was going on.

'Hello, boy,' Antonio said, clicking his fingers. The dog,

his tail wagging, trotted obediently over. 'Sorry I couldn't deliver him personally as I promised,' he said, patting the animal's head. 'I was called away unexpectedly.'

He had been about to leave when his sister had rung to say her youngest had been rushed into hospital with suspected appendicitis. She had three other children to care for, and with their mother on a world cruise and her husband in New York it had been time to call in a favour.

Sophia always had had perfect timing.

'Were you?' Fleur said, doing everything but yawn to silently signal her total lack of interest.

'Will you come?'

'So that you two won't have to talk to each other? I don't think so.'

'I'm not a woman.'

This comment brought Fleur's eyes back to his face. 'I'd noticed.'

Their eyes locked and suddenly the air was crackling with tension and alive with possibilities. The sort of possibilities that made her pulse rate quicken.

'And you are a woman.'

The tactile quality in his voice sent a shocking jolt of desire through her body. Fleur tensed and stepped backwards, her shoulder blades pressing into the door-frame.

'And Tamara might prefer a woman to shop with.'

Fleur, her expression schooled into blandness, stuck out her chin, determined not to let him see how his presence got to her even though she suspected it was way too late for such caution. Antonio Rochas had probably been born knowing the effect he had on women.

'I can't imagine that lingerie counters make you blush.' She licked her dry lips.

The action caught his attention. 'Do I make you nervous?'

She tried to sound amused as she retorted, 'You'd like that, wouldn't you?'

'You want to know what I would like?' The abrupt question had a driven quality.

Her throat thick with emotions she was reluctant to put a name to, Fleur shook her head. Antonio took a strand of pale hair that had fallen across her face, his expression distracted as he smoothed it back from her brow. Holding her wide eyes, he set one hand on the wall above her head. Her heart thudded as he leaned forward, his big body curving over her.

'But I think you know…and you would like it too, I think?' The insolent half-smile that lifted one corner of his fascinating mouth did not touch his eyes. They were bluer than the brightest summer sky. Blue, hot and hungry; it made her dizzy just to look at them.

Somehow Fleur forced the words past the limp in her aching throat. 'I think you should go.'

'I think so too,' he agreed, showing no sign of doing so.

'Well?' She raised a brow, but instead of achieving irony her smile managed to come across as a victim of blind, relentless lust, which was nothing but the truth.

'Have you any idea what it does to me to see you tremble just thinking about me touching you?' He appeared to expect no reply, which was just as well because Fleur's vocal cords were paralysed.

'Shall I tell you?' Antonio asked, touching a finger to the narrow band of midriff exposed where her tee shirt had ridden up.

Fleur gasped at the electric shock that sizzled all the way to her toes. She went to slap his hand away, but somehow she ended up holding on to his wrist. She expelled her breath on a shuddering sigh as his flexed fingers spread across her warm flesh.

Under his fingertips he could feel the contraction of the fine muscles just under the surface of her smooth belly. He watched as her delicate eyelids closed and pinkness washed over her skin until it glowed rosily.

He was stunned by how responsive she was to his lightest touch. His eyes darkened as his level of arousal hiked up several more painful notches.

Breathing in short, choppy bursts, she forced her eyes open. 'You can't do this...we can't do this...'

'Why not?' he asked, cupping the back of her head in his hand.

'Because your daughter might see us.'

The prospect did not appear to dampen his enthusiasm—at least it felt that way to Fleur as he placed a hand in the small of her back and pulled her hard up against him. 'That,' he said, fixing her with a hungry, burning stare, 'is what you do to me.'

Fleur managed to access the part of her brain that hadn't turned to mush and mumbled weakly, 'Tamara...'

'It would be more educational for her to catch us kissing than a sex-education lecture.'

'This isn't kissing!'

No sex-education lecture in the galaxy could have prepared me for an encounter with this man, Fleur thought, moaning softly as the hard imprint of his erection ground suggestively into her belly.

'It might also traumatise her for life. No child likes to think their parent is sexually active.'

'Sexually active? Not recently,' he muttered under his breath as he lowered his head to kiss her.

About an inch from making contact she turned her head. 'Please, Antonio...' she begged.

Torn between frustration and concern because she was

visibly shaking, Antonio stepped back. The hand he raised to drag the hair back from his brow was not quite steady.

Swallowing, Fleur lifted her eyes to his. The skin was pulled tight across the planes of his hard-boned face, suggesting a tension that was echoed in the unnatural rigidity of his lean body.

'Right, this isn't the time.'

'There is never going to be a right time. Or place.'

'Any place would suit me.'

The earthy admission made her shaky knees almost fold.

'Are you going to come with us?' he asked.

Fleur shook her head. 'I think you and Tamara need some time alone.'

'We have had some time alone.' He sketched a mirthless smile.

'And on any of those occasions, you stupid man, did you tell her that you care?'

'What did you say?'

'I said you're a stupid man, which you are.' Fleur spelt it out because for a man with a mind like a steel trap he could be extremely dense. 'Tamara thinks you don't care and you so obviously do. Would it kill you to tell her?' she asked him.

'Obviously I care.'

'Oh, for goodness' sake! Don't get on your high horse with me. The point that you seem to be missing—'

His lips quivered. 'Because I am a stupid man?'

'It isn't *obvious* to her, Antonio.' She caught his arm, her eyes widening fractionally as she felt the extreme tension in his muscles. In an urgent undertone, she added, 'She won't know you want her unless you tell her. *Go on...*' she urged.

Had he stood there looking so shocked on any other occasion she might have laughed. 'I thought you were supposed to be good at everything?' she taunted gently.

'So did I.' His expressive mouth twisted into a self-derisory smile and Fleur's fingers tightened on his arm. 'Meeting you has taught me otherwise.'

Fleur saw he was staring at her fingers curled around his sleeve and self-consciously let her hand fall clear.

'I have missed so much.'

'Missed?'

'Tamara growing up…I have no memories.'

The husky explanation made her eyes fill. 'It doesn't mean you can't build some memories.'

She saw him look startled by the suggestion, and then thoughtful.

'Sandy and I were just going for a walk.'

Fleur rattled the lead that was conveniently in her pocket and the dog appeared bang on cue at her side.

'But feel free to use my cottage if you want to talk—a neutral territory, sort of thing. Help yourself to tea and biscuits,' she added cheerily as she started to walk away.

She had gone only a dozen steps when Antonio's hand landed on her shoulder.

'What are you doing?' he asked.

'You and Tamara need some time alone…' Releasing an exasperated sigh, she twisted back and focused her frustrated frown on his face. 'You don't need me there. You two need to talk. Not later or tomorrow—you need to talk now. Just leave the key under the mat when you leave.'

His darkened eyes moved across her face, and just when she thought she couldn't withstand the searching, soul-stripping scrutiny a second longer without pleading guilty to something—actually *anything*—Antonio smiled.

'You really are an unusual woman,' he observed.

'Yes, I'm unique…so go talk to your daughter.' She looked pointedly at the hand that still lay heavily on her shoulder. Instead of letting go, he tightened his grip possessively.

'Looks like we're not going to make it to London and tomorrow I have to be in Paris, just for the day.'

'That's nice,' she said, wondering where he was going with this.

'But the next day, would you like to have dinner with me?'

Fleur's eyes widened. Obviously she was going to refuse, but it was rather nice to be asked.

'Well, it's nice of you to ask, but I'm… What would you do if I said no?'

'I would report your vicious dog to the appropriate authorities,' he said, deadpan.

Her lips quivered. 'Then this is blackmail?'

'If it makes you say yes, definitely.'

'Then I have no choice. What time will you pick me up?'

'Seven?'

'Seven-thirty.'

The last thing she saw before she turned away was the look of male triumph on his face.

'Sandy,' she told the animal at her side, 'I am an idiot.' Having established her insanity, she looked into the liquid canine eyes and asked, 'But what do you think I should wear? It's not good to overdress. I'm thinking sexy but not tarty and… Oh, God,' she sighed. 'I really am an idiot.'

CHAPTER TEN

THE next day Fleur got back from work around five. Opening the garden gate, she wandered up the path, pausing to pick a bunch of thyme to add to the casserole she planned to make later. She was sniffing the fragrant sprigs when she saw the figure sitting on her doorstep.

'Are you running away again or were you just passing?'

The girl grinned and got to her feet, dusting off the seat of her jeans. 'I was out for a walk.'

'With or without your father's permission?'

'I told *Antonio* I was going for a walk. He's not home today. He's gone to Paris or something.'

Fleur smiled and turned the key in the lock. His name made her think of the outfit laid out on her bed upstairs. After a great many twirls in front of the mirror she had finally decided on the midnight-blue velvet with the scalloped neckline that hinted at her cleavage and made her hips look frankly too good to be true.

'Do you want to come in?' she asked as Sandy exploded from the hallway all wagging tail and frantic barking. 'Be careful,' she cautioned. 'He licks.'

Tamara, who was stroking the excitable animal, nodded. 'I've been trying to ring my dad, the other one, but every time…' She stopped and, taking a deep breath, looked at

Fleur. 'He doesn't want me anymore, does he? It's not Antonio stopping him? Look, Fleur, if you know, I need you to tell me…I'm not a kid…I have a right.'

'You should ask your father…Antonio. It's not my place…'

'Do you think I haven't tried?' she asked, following Fleur inside the cottage. 'Have you any idea how good he is at *not* answering a question?'

Fleur flicked the switch on the electric kettle and turned back to her youthful guest. 'What has happened to make you think…?'

'That dear Dad isn't waging a legal battle to get me back?' the girl inserted, shrugging. 'I was exploring yesterday and I found all my stuff from home boxed up…absolutely everything, and I mean everything. Baby photos, the lot.'

'I expect he thought you might need your things…that you'd feel more comfortable with them around you,' Fleur suggested lamely.

'It's more like he's wiping me out of his life. Every time I ring his office they say he's unavailable and our home number comes up as number unrecognised.' She looked at Fleur with eyes that seemed far older than her years and said, 'I'm right, aren't I? He dumped me on Antonio.

'Please tell me, Fleur. I'm sick of nobody giving me a straight answer. I *need* to know, I really do…I go back to school tomorrow and I need to know if it's worth coming home for weekends. If Antonio really wants me to come home.'

Put on the spot, Fleur didn't have the faintest idea what to do. She thought the girl deserved the truth, but she respected and understood Antonio's decision to protect her. 'What makes you think I know anything?' she prevaricated.

'I know if Antonio was going to tell anyone it would be you.'

This confident assertion made Fleur blink. 'Tamara, I think you might have the wrong idea. I hardly know your father.'

'But he did tell you, didn't he?'

Fleur inhaled deeply and, unable to resist the appeal in the girl's eyes any longer, reluctantly nodded. 'I think that is how it happened. Try not to think too badly of your other father.' The pathetic creep. 'I expect he was hurt to learn that you weren't his. People do crazy things when they're hurt.' As if this girl didn't know all about hurting.

'Relieved, more like. Still, it's no big loss.'

Fleur's heart ached for the girl as she tried to put a brave face on it. 'I'm sure that's not true,' she lied. 'He probably acted on impulse and I'm sure he'll regret it.'

'He and Mum weren't exactly kid people,' Tamara revealed. 'Until I went to school I saw more of my nanny than them. You know, she'd have me pretend I was younger than I was to her friends—until I grew too tall, that is. She hated me being tall.'

These casual revelations horrified Fleur, who had enjoyed a happy, carefree childhood to the core.

'And now Antonio is stuck with me.'

'He doesn't think of it that way,' Fleur said with total conviction.

'He did say he wanted me around,' the girl admitted. 'He says he wants to make it official, have me take his name and everything.'

'And how do you feel about that?'

'I don't know…he says it's up to me.'

'Family is ultra important to Spaniards.'

'Really? I thought that was just, you know, in books and films and things.'

Fleur shook her head and offered the reassurance she sensed the girl was asking for. 'No, it's not just in films. I think you've got a family whether you want one or not.'

'He's awfully bossy.'

Fleur nodded.

'And all my friends at school will have crushes on him, which will be *extremely* embarrassing.'

'I wouldn't be at all surprised.'

'You think I should give him a chance, don't you?'

'Does it matter what I think?'

'Well, he likes you.'

Fleur told herself that it would be juvenile and foolish to feel pleased. And felt pleased anyway. 'My dog bit him,' she confided. 'About thirty seconds after we met.'

A giggle escaped a wide-eyed Tamara. *'Honestly?'*

Fleur shook her head. 'As first impressions go it takes some beating.'

The grave pronouncement sent the teenager into fits of laughter.

'But Sandy loves him now.' There's a lot of it about.

'He is very…'

'Charismatic?' Fleur suggested.

Tamara nodded with enthusiasm. She glanced at her watch. 'He said he'd ring around six, you know,' she said casually. 'I might make my way back home.' At the door she turned with an impish grin. 'Shall I give him your love? Or would you prefer to give him that yourself?' Laughing, she left a red-faced Fleur staring after her. Out of the mouths of babes!

The journey along the minor roads took ten minutes. It probably ought to have taken a little longer, but Antonio was in a hurry.

When he arrived he discovered that the college consisted of several buildings sprawled over quite a large area, all red brick and none very inspiring to look at. Not that Antonio, who parked his Mercedes in front of the main building, was thinking about architectural merits.

He only had himself to blame and he knew it. He had trusted her, first mistake. You trusted a woman and you deserved what you got. Expect the worst of people and occasionally you were pleasantly surprised. It was a philosophy that had got him this far…and look what happened when he abandoned it!

Give something of himself, Sophia had said. It just showed how much, or in this case now *little*, his sister knew!

Fleur added the last mark to the list of grades with a sigh of relief, satisfied she had used her free period to good effect. Now she would have all evening to make herself look gorgeous. She was sliding the stack of papers into her bag when the door banged open without warning to reveal a tall and very angry figure.

Actually, *angry* did not do justice to the raw fury that the unannounced intruder was vibrating with. Jaw clenched, nostrils flared, his patrician features tautened another notch as he stepped fully into the room. His expression had a windchill factor of minus thirty.

A combination of shock and confusion held Fleur immobile while she tried to figure why on earth he was here.

'I thought our date was tonight?'

'How dare you interfere in what does not concern you?' Antonio's low voice had the sort of carrying quality that any member of her classes would have been proud to reproduce. And such was his tall, commanding presence that he would only have to walk onto a stage to have the audience fall under his spell.

The normally faint foreign inflection in Antonio's voice was very pronounced as he raised a sardonic brow and added. 'I am waiting.'

Prodded into action, Fleur closed her jaw with an audible snap. 'I have a class in five minutes.'

'And I, Ms Stewart, have a problem, and that problem,' he said, 'is you!'

As she walked past him to close the door, acting as though he weren't there, her slender back stiff, her chin lifted to a disdainful angle, Antonio's control remained intact, but only just. He considered himself a pretty good judge of human character, but the problem was for the first time since he was a teenager he had allowed old-fashioned lust to cloud his judgement.

But could lust alone explain the bizarre fact that he seemed to rip his soul bare if he was in her company for more than two minutes at a stretch? It was the modern fashion, he knew, to dissect your emotions and analyse your motivation to the point where you could not blink without it being a product of a childhood trauma.

But that was not his way.

There was a handful of people outside his family Antonio trusted, trusted with his life, but it would never have occurred to him to unburden his worries on them. And they would not expect it; his friends were the sort of people who respected his reserved nature.

This woman respected nothing, certainly not him.

'Do I get a clue?' she wondered, leaning back against the closed door. Her breath coming in short, choppy bursts, Fleur fought to contain her anger. 'No, don't tell me. I don't want to know. I just want you to go. Just how dare you?'

'How dare I?

His sneering tone sent a fresh wave of anger through her tense body. 'Look, if you think I'm going to stand here and play whipping boy for you, you're dead wrong. If you've got a problem with something I have done, you can tell it to my answering machine.'

He bared his teeth in a savage smile. 'Oh, I have a problem.' He had a problem with her mouth and the overpowering need he was experiencing to cover it with his own.

'This is my place of work. How would you like it if I barged into your office and started yelling the odds?'

Had it even occurred to him that if anyone had seen or heard him she would be getting the fallout from this little stunt for the next six months? Of course it hadn't, because he had never considered anyone else in his life!

'I am not yelling. You are.'

Infuriatingly, he was right. Fleur compressed her lips and tried to regain control of her tumultuous breathing.

'How did you know where I was?'

'I asked someone.'

Fleur buried her face in her hands and groaned.

This got worse!

There was no chance at all that no one had recognised him. Antonio Rochas changed his hairstyle and it was national news!

Occasionally the private life of staff intruded into the workplace and it became the subject of speculation amongst her colleagues and the student population. The idea of being the subject of staff-room gossip made Fleur feel nauseous.

'You knew that I did not want Tamara to know about Finch. You knew my wishes, but you decided to ignore them. Why would you do that? Other than this natural desire you appear to have to flaunt my authority?'

Fleur's jaw dropped. 'You're saying this is about me answering Tamara's questions.' Actually she knew it wasn't. It was clear to Fleur that this was about establishing some ground rules. This was about her stepping over some invisible line that women he wanted to sleep with were not allowed within fifty feet of.

She'd already been in one unequal relationship. A shiver ran down her spine when she thought about how close she'd come to walking into another.

'Your authority!' she choked. 'You don't have any—not over me, anyway. I'm quite capable of making my own judgements. You're not my father!'

'No, but I am Tamara's.'

'And she has my sympathy!' Fleur flared.

He flinched.

'I do not pretend to be a perfect father,' he retorted grimly.

'You don't have to be *perfect*…but maybe *you* do? Perhaps that's your problem. You want to be the best at everything?'

Antonio's lips curled as he looked down into her wide-spaced golden eyes. 'I am not interested in your psycho-babble theories. I have no idea what your motivation was when you told Tamara about her father. But I can guess—'

'*You're* her father.'

The soft interruption made Antonio pause, but his tone had not softened when he broke the taut silence. 'A fact you decided to ignore when you went against my express wishes,' he reminded her.

'I can see how it might seem that way to someone as autocratic as you,' Fleur conceded.

'I am not autocratic!'

This blast drew an audible giggle from the corridor outside. Fleur grimaced and stifled a groan of horror; the walls in the building were paper-thin. A fact she really ought to have kept in mind before taking part in a slanging match.

'Will you lower your voice?' she begged in a hushed undertone. 'I'm not trying to deny I told Tamara that the no-contact situation wasn't your idea. But when she came to me she already knew. She's not stupid; she had worked it out. What was I meant to do? Lie when she asked me?' Even as she spoke she knew that he wasn't hearing a word she was saying.

'I have to tell you, if this was your way of ingratiating yourself—'

The furrows on her smooth brow deepened. '*Ingratiate*? I don't know what you're talking about.'

One dark brow lifted. 'No?'

'No, I don't.'

'Then let me spell it out. You create a problem and then step in to heal it. '

Fleur blinked, totally bewildered by the angry assertion. 'Why on earth would I do that?'

'To use the influence you appear to wield over my daughter to worm your way into my life…make yourself indispensable—'

Her jaw dropped in shock. 'Your life!' she echoed in a stunned voice. 'What are you talking about?'

Antonio ignored her bewildered question. 'You pretend you care about her.' And he had not just let her into their lives, he had actively nourished the connection.

A flash of angry colour travelled up Fleur's neck until her pale cheeks grew hot. 'I do care about her.'

'You sound sincere, but then sincerity is your forte, isn't it, Fleur? Sincere and sweet and a great listener…' And he had fallen for it all, the phoney concern, the caring eyes, he thought, his lips curling into a grim smile of self-disgust. And how, how had he forgotten that women always wanted something, they always had an agenda? Maybe it was because he hadn't been thinking with his head, but areas much farther south!

'You think I used Tamara because I wanted…I wanted to be part of your life? You think I want to be part of your magic circle?' She swallowed and loosed a low-pitched, ironic laugh. Well, at least she knew what he thought of her.

'You think this is funny?'

'Funny! My God, if I'm ever as cynical as you I hope someone puts me out of my misery. I knew you thought a lot of yourself, but even for you this must be a new high. I hate to blow your lovely conspiracy theory sky-high, but I really don't go home at night and think about how to get myself a billionaire. People generally don't.'

Antonio, who had been the target for unscrupulous and often inventive campaigns over the years, raised a brow and said sardonically, 'You don't think so?'

'Oh, poor you!' she drawled with insincere sympathy. 'I suppose you have to fight them off with a stick. Do you work on the theory that every woman you meet wants your body…or is it your bank account, not your integrity, you're worried about preserving? Oh, yes, I'd love a chunk of your money because I can see how damned happy it makes you.'

An expression of total astonishment chased across his patrician features. 'You are trying to tell me you feel sorry for me?'

'No, I save my pity for people who deserve it.'

The biting retort made his jaw tighten another notch. 'And money means nothing to you, I suppose.'

Fleur considered the jeering question seriously. 'Of course it does. It's nice to feel secure and have nice things sometimes, but all money does—or at least the amount you have—is complicate things. Women do want other things, you know. We're not all grasping sluts. Some of us can manage without millions in the bank and haven't even had sex for two years…' She stopped, all expression blanking from her face as the awful words hung in the air.

She'd have given anything to have retrieved them, but she couldn't. They were out there doing all manner of damage to her self-esteem, not to mention her moral authority.

I did not say that. *Please* tell me I did not say that, she prayed silently.

But of course she had. The mother and grandfather of all Freudian slips and it was all hers. This was a situation where damage limitation was the best she could hope for.

'Two years is a long time.'

Tell me about it, she thought, maintaining a tight-lipped silence in the face of his glittery-eyed scrutiny.

'So you don't want my money, just my body.'

Fleur cast him a look of intense dislike. 'That was a figure of speech…'

'No, that was a cry from the heart.'

'My heart has nothing to do with this.'

'You want me as much as I want you.'

Fleur's teeth clenched as she heard the smug inflection in his voice. She wanted to scream with sheer frustration. She had done what she had sworn she would never do again, she had revealed her vulnerability.

'Hormones, not heart!' she snarled. 'And get that look off your face. I wouldn't have you if you came gift-wrapped!'

Unwrapping the parcel might be fun, though. The forbidden thought brought a fresh prickle of heat to her skin.

Her jaw clenched as she faced him with all the aggression of a small, cornered animal.

'I like my life the way it is. Why the hell would I want to have any part of yours, or, for that matter, you? In case you hadn't noticed, Antonio, you've got baggage.'

'And you are one of those women who consider a family an undesirable encumbrance?'

His hypocrisy was more than she could bear. 'This from the man who hasn't stopped for one second since he learnt he was a father to appreciate how damned lucky he is.'

Antonio looked startled. '*Lucky…?*'

'Yes, lucky. So very, *very* lucky.' She felt her eyes fill and blinked angrily.

Antonio saw the tears and frowned. He knew there was something he was missing, but he knew when to keep quiet.

The words continued to spill from her. 'A child may not fit

in with your playboy image, but some people would envy you. Do you have any idea how many people would love to be in your position?' she demanded. 'You may have lost out on Tamara's early years, but you have her now.

'If you're not totally stupid and blow it completely, she'll be part of your life for the foreseeable future. Do you know how lucky that makes you in my book?' she raged. 'People like you who don't appreciate what they have really make me mad!'

She dabbed the back of her hand angrily to brush away the tears sliding down her cheeks. 'How many people want a family and can't have one? How many people have a f-family and lose him…?'

Crying in earnest now, she covered her mouth with her hand and closed her eyes tight. The painful sound of her choked sobs filled the awful silence as it stretched.

'Who did you lose, Fleur?'

'I had a miscarriage…'

Antonio had never experienced a mood swing so swift or drastic. He looked at her bowed head and experienced the most overwhelming desire to make her stop hurting.

'It was a difficult pregnancy…apparently these things happen for no reason sometimes,' she explained, accepting the handkerchief that was pushed into her hand.

Their eyes met and she saw enormous compassion, which Fleur's defensive mechanisms translated as pity.

Pity was the one thing she couldn't, *wouldn't,* take! She took one enormous gulping breath and tried to feign calm. Inside she was a breath away from completely losing it.

'It was eighteen months ago, and I don't want to talk about it.'

He studied her face in silence for a moment and then almost imperceptibly nodded. 'Fine,' he said, 'then let's get back to a subject close to both of our hearts…sex.'

'I don't believe you; you're such a callous opportunist!' she cried.

'You didn't want my sympathy. I'm only offering what you do want. Don't you think it's ever so slightly childish under the circumstances to pretend that we don't both need to get this thing out our systems?'

'Oh, my, the romance!' she gushed sarcastically. 'The old-fashioned charm that is so absent from modern life. Now I know why no woman can resist you.' She threw him a look of total contempt and stalked out of the room.

CHAPTER ELEVEN

A COUPLE of eager students had stayed behind at the end of the last session of the day to ask Fleur's advice. Normally she was only too happy to put in extra time, but today she wanted to go home and escape all the curious eyes.

By the time she finally made it to the staff car park hers was the only car left. She dug into the pockets of her coat and came up empty, so, shoving her bag on one hip, she scrabbled inside for her elusive car keys and discovered everything but. Impatient, she resorted to emptying the entire contents of her capacious bag on the top of the car bonnet and almost immediately saw her keyring—saw it a second before it slid to the ground and then in slow motion vanished down the grating of a drain.

Fleur lifted her hands to her head and released a cry of sheer disbelief before dropping down to her knees, oblivious to the fact her coat was dragging on the wet ground. Through the grating she could see what might have been the glint of metal. She tried to move the heavy covering, but accepted it was futile after a few seconds. The darned thing was lodged tight.

She brushed her grubby fingers together and sat back on her heels.

'Great, the perfect end to a perfect day!' She heaved a sigh and felt the prickle of self-pitying tears sting her eyelids. 'Someone really doesn't like me—' She broke off as a pair of shiny shoes came into view.

And here was someone else who didn't like her.

'Are you stalking me?' She had to raise her voice above the deafening thud of her accelerated heartbeat.

'I have come to apologise.'

Breathless excitement was not the reaction of a sane person to the voice of a man she loathed. But then sanity had nothing to do with the things she felt around Antonio!

'Apology accepted, now go away,' she grunted without lifting her eyes from foot level.

'Earlier—'

'Does the word grapevine mean anything to you? Have you any idea of how many versions of *earlier* are circulating by now? Until today when I walked down the corridor nobody stared or whispered.' Actually not everyone was whispering! 'And I have to tell you that was the way I liked it. Living your life in a goldfish bowl may appeal to you, but some of us enjoy our privacy.'

An expression of incredulous disbelief washed over Antonio's face as he stared at the top of her silky head. In his experience women were all too aware of the effect they had on the opposite sex.

'If you thought you ever faded into the background you are totally deluded.' His hands clenched at his sides as he visualised those anonymous eyes covetously following her every move.

The tug Fleur had been fighting became impossible to resist, and her eyes were drawn upwards until they reached his dark face. Back-lit by the hard pale light of the overhead security light, his face looked all fascinating angles and intriguing hollows.

He looked dangerous and complicated and sinfully gorgeous—he was all three. Their eyes locked and a sharp illicit thrill chased along her receptive nerve endings.

Her throat felt achy and raw as she protested, 'I'm not deluded!'

'You're—!' His eyes slid from hers. 'Fine, you're not deluded,' he acceded, sounding as if he was bored with the entire subject.

His patronising attitude really got under Fleur's skin. 'Don't humour me. I'm not a child.'

'But if you're not deluded you just live in some sort of alternative universe.' He subjected her face to a feature-by-feature inspection before explaining in a husky voice that sent a tingle all the way down to her toes, 'Because, believe me, in this world men do not *not* notice a woman who looks the way you do.'

'I'm ordinary,' she protested.

'Your skin is totally flawless.' Fleur froze as he squatted down to her level. Her eyes half closed as he ran his finger down the curve of her cheek. 'And,' he rasped in a mesmerising whisper, 'like silk.'

'Very funny.' Her breath coming in a series of choky, uneven little gasps, she turned her head to break the debilitating contact.

'Have I mentioned your mouth?'

His voice gave a whole new meaning to seductive; the husky rasp was positively sinful. Her eyelashes lifted off her cheeks as she directed a defiant look at him.

She touched her fingers to her lips, exhilarated and scared all at once, and heard herself ask, 'What's wrong with my mouth?'

She felt rather than heard the primal rumble in his chest as he inhaled sharply and answered huskily, 'Not a thing.'

Before she had time to do anything but lift her passion-glazed eyes to his he suddenly stiffened and barked, 'Get up! *Por Dios*, woman, I'm not made of stone. I can't think with you down there. Or, rather,' he added with a self-derisive sneer, 'I can think.'

Her mind computed the thing he might be thinking and her inner temperature jumped by several degrees.

Her eyes widened in protest as he grabbed her arm and hauled her bodily to her feet. Gritting her teeth, Fleur looked pointedly from his face to the fingers encircling her upper arm and back again. He ignored the message.

'I've apologized. What do you want me to do?' he demanded.

Kissing me would be good. As she looked at his mouth things inside her melted some more. So don't look! Her lashes came down over her eyes as she tore her eyes from the sensual curve of his lips. It was time she took back some control.

Fleur couldn't fight him *and* her own compulsion to lean into him, to let her body melt into his hardness. So she let his fingers stay where they were and tried not to think about the heat of his sleek, hard male body.

'Going away would be good, for starters,' she returned, her voice as cool as her body was hot. 'After all, there is no one around and half the fun of calling someone a calculating bitch is having people hear you do it.'

In the shadows the colour along his chiselled cheek-bones deepened.

'I spoke with Tamara…'

'Great! Though,' she added bitterly, 'it might have been even *greater* if you'd done that before you barged in accusing me—'

'She explained things more clearly.'

'The way I tried to. I suppose she tried to as well, but you probably didn't listen to her any more than you listened to me. You heard what you wanted to and you wanted to believe that I'm a conniving bitch. What's wrong, Antonio—was I getting too close?'

Fleur, who was staring fixedly at the floor, did not see his face as her shot in the dark hit home.

'I do not—' He broke off, loosing an impatient curse as he cupped her chin in one hand and dragged her face up towards his. 'It is very difficult to talk to the top of someone's head.' His eyes flickered to her head as he lifted a section of silky blonde hair from her nape and let it slide through his long brown fingers.

His lips quirked into a quick self-derisive smile as he let his hand fall away. It came to rest on the curve of her hip.

If anyone saw them they would look like lovers embracing. The shocking idea sent a shameful rush of heat through Fleur's body. She released the breath trapped in her lungs in a series of controlled little gasps and told herself firmly, This has to stop!

'As I was *trying* to say, I do not always act as rationally around you as I might.' She heard the sardonic inflection in his voice and heard him add in an odd voice, 'But then we both know why that is...so I might have overreacted.'

'*Might...?* You think?' The puzzled expression in her eyes deepened. 'What do we both know?'

'We both know that it's not easy to maintain objectivity when you're dealing with someone you can't look at without thinking about being in bed naked with them.'

The colour flew to Fleur's cheeks. '*Naked?*' she echoed in a strangled squeak.

'That is my normal condition when I am in bed with a beautiful woman.'

'I do not want to hear about your other women.' Then, realising that her words might be interpreted as an admission that she was one of them, she hastily added, 'Poor, misguided idiots—they have my deepest sympathy.'

'I don't want to talk about any woman but you. I don't want any woman but you. Do not pretend you don't know what I'm saying. That you haven't thought about these things too.'

'Are you implying I think about you naked?'

'Are you saying you don't?'

Fleur decided it was a lot wiser not to go there. 'My God, you think everything is about sex.'

'Not everything, but with you it's not something that is easy to think past.'

'I suppose you think I'm going to find your candour endearing.'

'You really think that I'm in any condition to be calculating.' He vented a hoarse laugh. 'I can't function at even a basic level. You're…' He shook his head. 'I just don't have the vocabulary to describe what you're doing to me.'

Their eyes locked and suddenly all Fleur's anger and resentment died. 'You're making my life pretty miserable too,' she confided huskily.

'Then what do you suggest we do about it, *querida*?'

Close to tears, she shook her head. 'We can't do anything. This thing is totally doomed before it's even started. You don't really trust me. *I* don't really trust me. I don't do casual relationships; you don't do anything else.'

Incredulity stamped on his dark features, he asked, 'Are you telling me you are hanging out for a ring?'

'Do I look that stupid?' she asked. 'We're talking about sex…and you don't marry someone for sex.' You marry for love, or she did, but it seemed her own personal doom was she had fallen for a man who was never going to love her back.

'I'd like to do more than talk.'

Fleur, ignoring the growled insert, allowed her eyes to slide from his.

'You marry someone for things that last, and, besides, I just…well, the thing is I'm not actually very…well, good at sex, and I can live without it. And I think—' She stopped midsentence as his hands suddenly closed around her upper arms.

'You can live without sex?' he practically yelled, yanking her roughly towards him.

Collapsing with a gasp against his chest, she lifted her face to his. 'It works for me,' she contended stubbornly.

'I didn't think it possible…' he observed, pinning her with a scalpel-like glare; he swallowed, the contraction of the muscles in his brown throat visible as he completed his scathing denunciation '…that any female could be as stupid as you are.'

'I am just being practical!' she protested, struggling to sever the almost hypnotic hold of his burning blue glare.

'Practical,' he sneered. 'You don't need practical, you need me!' Before she could refute this outrageous contention his mouth came crashing down on hers hard, hungry and devastatingly skilful.

After the first nanosecond of resistance Fleur melted into him. Her mind and body were so attuned to the man who ruthlessly plundered her lips that she had no idea where he began and she ended.

It was a kiss that seared her senses. And when it was gone she had been reduced to a seething mass of shredded nerve endings and inarticulate longing.

Eyes locked blue on amber, the silence between them stretched until finally Antonio took her by the shoulders and put her physically away from him.

'I suggest,' he said as he turned away, 'that you go home and think about what you can really live without because, take my word for it,' he assured her, dragging a hand across his own mouth, 'it's not sex.'

It wasn't until she heard a distant engine roar into life that Fleur realised she had no means of getting home and even less means of thinking.

'I suppose this means our date is off?' she said to thin air.

CHAPTER TWELVE

ANTONIO nodded as he walked past the contractors who had arrived that morning to bring some order to the area of sadly neglected woodland. He had walked on a hundred yards or so before the few stray words he had unconsciously picked up registered.

Face set, he turned back. The men who were eating their packed lunches fell silent as he approached

He arched an enquiring brow. 'A fire, you said? Near the church?'

The older man of the group nodded. 'Yeah, that little cottage just down the lane. Sold last year to an outsider. The place is completely gutted apparently.'

'Was anyone hurt?'

To Antonio's complete frustration nobody could tell him. His pace quickened as he headed in a homeward direction; a few hundred yards down the track he broke into a run.

The fire crews had gone.

Had she left a candle burning in the bedroom? they had asked. Fleur had had to guiltily concede that it was possible. The roof was still in too unstable a state for them to confirm their suspicions.

She was sitting in the remnants of her herb garden when her mobile phone rang.

'Hi, Mum, yes, I'm fine. How is Dad? Great…do you mind awfully if I ring you back? Someone is at the door.' Actually I have no door, she thought, looking at the charred remains as she slid the phone back into her pocket. 'Sandy, I think we are homeless.'

Sandy wagged his tail and Fleur envied his state of blissful ignorance. The fire crew had advised she contact her insurers as soon as possible. Good advice, except Fleur wasn't sure who they were and she was pretty sure that the information she needed had probably gone up in the fire.

'You have to put things in perspective, Sandy,' she told her companion. 'This is bad, but nobody was hurt so it's not a tragedy.'

'I admire your philosophical attitude.'

Fleur leapt a foot off the ground and spun around a full one hundred and eighty degrees. *'You…!'* she gasped.

'Your face is black.'

'Yes, I should think so,' she agreed, absently lifting a hand to her cheek and in the process adding another streak. 'I thought Sandy was inside and I tried…but the smoke was…' She stopped, closed her eyes and took a deep breath. When she cautiously opened them again Antonio was still there; he was not some spectre conjured by her wishful thinking. 'But Sandy wasn't inside, so it was fine.'

The firefighter who had pulled her out of the burning building had been pretty scathing about her mercy dash and in the clear light of day Fleur couldn't really blame him.

'Fine, aside from the fact my house has burnt down… though the fire crew said it could have been worse. The roof is bad and there's a lot of smoke damage inside, but they did say that it could have been a lot worse and they should know.

You have to keep these things in perspective… Have I already said that? Am I babbling?'

'Yes.'

His stunning eyes were so warm that she wanted to cry.

She turned her head away. Her house had burnt down and she had kept it together; Antonio looked sorry for her and she wanted to wail like a banshee. It was not rational. Hopefully the insanity was temporary, yet she realised at that moment with total certainty that her feelings for him were not.

When she turned her head she saw he was staring at the burnt-out building. His expression was grim.

'They think it was a candle. I left a candle burning in the bedroom. It was scented, lavender. Lavender is meant to relax you, only not on this occasion.' One step short of hysterics, she bit her lip.

The stupidity of her comments invited a cutting comeback and yet somehow none was forthcoming.

Actually, now that she thought about it, Antonio was looking a little…*odd*, himself. Though odd in a perfectly sensationally sexy way as opposed to babbling-like-an-idiot odd.

'Did you hear the sirens? Is that why you're here?' Antonio had never struck her as the sort of person who stood around watching accidents. 'They were really very prompt. Firemen are pretty marvelous, you know.' She stopped and swallowed. 'Actually,' she confessed, 'I'm really not sure what I'm meant to do next.'

'You're meant to come home with me.'

'I don't think so…' He opened his arms and she added thickly as she walked into them, 'But I think I will anyway.'

He stroked her hair and said husky things in deep, vibrant Spanish while she clung to him and sobbed her heart out. There was something awfully liberating about letting go after what seemed like a lifetime of holding it in.

His chest had a comforting solidity and even when the emotional storm had passed she felt strangely reluctant to move from its immediate proximity, but the point came when she knew that for practical purposes she had to stop acting as if she'd been superglued to him.

'Sorry about that.' She lifted her head and pulled away; his arms immediately dropped. Feeling strangely bereft outside that magic circle, Fleur shivered.

'You have nothing to apologise for.'

'I'm not normally a *crying* sort of person.'

'You're not alone. As a race the British are on the whole emotionally inhibited.'

'Not today.' If she looked at the smoking remains of her lovely little home she knew she'd lose it again. 'It's odd,' she observed, wrapping her arms around herself as her teeth jarred against one another. 'I can't seem to stop shaking.'

With a soft curse he pulled off the sweater he wore. 'It's called shock,' he said as he pulled it over her head. It reached her knees. He rolled up the sleeves, then stepped back to view the results of his efforts.

She knew she must look like a clown, but he wasn't laughing.

His sweater was warm and soft. 'You'll get cold,' she protested, her nostrils flaring as she inhaled the unique fragrance held in the soft weave.

'No, I'm warm,' he said. 'Feel,' he invited, taking her hand and placing it against his chest.

Her stomach muscles promptly went into spasm.

'Yes, you are warm,' she admitted, her hands pressed into the solid wall of warm male muscle. 'I really should call the insurance company,' she observed vaguely.

His hands came up to cover her own, which still lay pressed flat against his chest. 'All in good time,' he said, using the sort of tone people reserved for fractious children.

or highly strung horses. 'Right now I think you should come with me.'

She tilted her head back to look into his face. 'You were serious about that—?'

'Which do you doubt—my sincerity or my motives?'

The question made Fleur feel mean and churlish.

'You fear for your virtue under my roof.'

'Looking like this!' She gestured downwards and laughed.

He didn't. He just carried on staring until finally she felt she had to break the painful silence.

'I just don't want to be a bother,' she explained awkwardly. 'But I must admit I would appreciate somewhere to stay tonight. I would go to a bed and breakfast but they don't all take dogs. Obviously I'll make other arrangements tomorrow.'

'Let's let tomorrow take care of itself, shall we?'

Fleur, who had been hit by a wave of exhaustion, making it made it a struggle just to stay on her feet, recognised that this happy-go-lucky policy didn't sound like the Antonio Rochas she knew, but she was too weary to make the observation out loud. She didn't even protest when he placed a hand under her elbow to support her as he led her to his car.

'Fasten your belt.'

'The dog—he's going to make a mess of your lovely upholstery.'

Antonio looked into her dazed eyes and smiled. 'I'll bill you,' he promised softly.

As he leaned across her to fasten her seat belt Fleur closed her eyes. 'You smell really nice. I didn't really say that, did I? I expect I smell of smoke. There was a lot of smoke.'

'Close your eyes.'

She laughed a little at the suggestion. 'I can't possibly fall asleep; there's too much to sort out.'

Actually she did fall asleep and even when she awoke she felt strangely disconnected from what was happening around her. She smiled, she said thank you…several times. She became tearful when people were nice and kind to her. She mechanically ate the food put in front of her when urged to do so by Antonio. All the while she had the strangest sense of being a spectator, watching things happen, rather than participating.

Much later that evening she was tucked up in bed when the door opened and Tamara crept in.

'You're not asleep, are you?' she asked in a whisper. 'Because if I woke you he'll probably ground me until I'm fifty.'

Fleur propped herself up on her elbow and immediately assured Tamara that she was totally awake.

'He was sleeping in my room but I just thought you might like him…good boy…' Encouraged by her enthusiastic patting of the bed, Sandy leapt up. 'I thought maybe,' Tamara said, smiling as the dog licked a protesting Fleur's face, 'you might want to have him around.'

Fleur was touched by the gesture. 'Yes, I would, thanks. What time is it?'

'About nine-thirty.'

Fleur began to struggle upright. 'I should get—'

'No, you shouldn't and if…anyone…finds out I woke you I'll be in big trouble.' The inflection in her voice when she said *anyone* made it obvious she was talking about Antonio.

'Well, I wouldn't want to get you in trouble.'

'No,' the girl agreed, a flicker of humour crossing her face. 'I can do that all by myself. Well, I'll let you sleep, then; if he catches me I really am history,' she said, making for the door. Her hand curved around the handle, she turned back. 'I'm really sorry about the fire, but I'm glad you're all right.'

'Me too,' Fleur said. 'And thanks,' she added, her glance sliding towards the dog who was making himself at home on the end of the bed.

* * *

Fleur pushed the door; it swung inwards silently.

She took a deep breath, and thought, If this is the wrong room I'm going to look pretty silly.

Actually there was a good chance that she'd look pretty silly even if it *was* the right room. It wasn't that she was totally crazy—a portion of her mind still retained some sanity—she just wasn't listening to what it was telling her. She knew he could never love her as he had loved Tamara's mother, but he wasn't completely indifferent to her, was he?

After all, she could be reading far too much into a couple of kisses and a few smouldering looks. He said he wanted her, but men notoriously said things they didn't mean in the heat of the moment, and maybe that moment and the heat had passed? Maybe smouldering was the norm for Antonio with any woman he was around?

If he wasn't consumed with lust the way she was—only quite obviously to a lesser degree because nobody had ever, *ever* wanted anyone as much as she wanted Antonio Rochas—she was setting herself up for some pretty major rejection here.

But then that was a risk she had decided was worth taking. The alternative was not following her instincts, not doing anything and never knowing.

The room she entered was big, lit at that moment by a single lamp set on a bureau. Other than the few striking modern paintings hanging on the pale painted walls, there were no decorative flourishes. It was borderline ascetic, just a few pieces of contemporary bespoke oak furniture and some vibrant rugs on the polished wood floor.

The heavy drapes were not pulled across the big floor-length windows where Antonio stood, his tall silhouette outlined against the night sky.

The image of him standing there staring out into the night burned itself in her consciousness.

Heart beating heavily in her breast, she took advantage of the moment to stare. Her glance lingered on his sternly beautiful profile before moving down the strong column of his neck and, lower still, skimming over his incredible athlete's body, its strength not concealed by the loosely tied robe he wore.

He was the iconic image of male beauty, but there was nothing aesthetic about the appreciation that curled like a tight fist in her belly. It was raw, primitive feelings he stirred inside her. Feelings that she hadn't even known she was capable of, just as she hadn't known she was capable of walking into a man's room in the middle of the night and offering herself to him.

The full impact of her reckless, wanton strategy was hitting home when he turned his head.

She froze like an animal caught in the headlights of a car.

He saw her and something flickered at the back of his eyes, something hot and fierce that sent her stomach into a diving lurch.

He didn't look surprised.

It was almost, Fleur thought, as if he had been expecting her, which was crazy because she hadn't known she was coming until five minutes ago. Maybe like her he felt at some instinctive level that this was meant to happen.

'I saw a light…' What she didn't add was that she had gone looking for it. But it seemed a fairly safe bet that he already knew that. 'You're not asleep.'

For some reason he appeared to find this comment amusing. The laughter didn't reach his eyes. The tension she saw in them was echoed in the rigidity of his stance. He dragged a hand across his shadowed jaw, his expression wary rather than welcoming.

Fleur looked at the dark shadow and her fingertips started to tingle as she imagined running her own fingers along that strong curve. How would it feel against other parts of her body?

'And your hair's wet.' She couldn't take her eyes from the single drop of water that was sliding down his tanned neck.

'I have just taken a shower.' The corners of his mouth lifted, but there was no lessening of the tension that drew the skin tight across his cheekbones.

'It's late to be taking a shower.' It was also late to leave your bed and go walkabout.

'A cold shower,' he elaborated.

She caught her breath sharply at this first encouraging signal. 'Did it work?' As she spoke her eyes slid downwards. It wasn't until she registered the answer to her question that she hastily dragged them upwards.

'As you see, not particularly well.' His grin broadened as her blush deepened. 'I was showering while you have been stumbling, sleepy-eyed, around the house?'

Actually there was nothing sleepy about the expression in her wide-spaced eyes. Determination and recklessness gleamed in those shimmering depths, but underlying all that there was a hunger that Antonio could readily identify with.

Her chin went up to a defiant angle. 'I know exactly what I'm doing. I didn't sleepwalk my way here. I thought about it very carefully.'

'The thoughts we have at two am in the morning are not always to be trusted.' His own could very well get him arrested! With her glorious hair tumbling around her face, she looked like a beautiful, wanton temptress.

'I woke up and I realised I could have died tonight. Do you realise that...?'

The blood left Antonio's knuckles as his hands clenched at

his sides. 'I did realise that.' *Realising that* was going to be the reason he woke up in a cold sweat for the next fifty years or so.

'It makes you think…you never know what's going to happen.'

This maddeningly elusive woman walking into his room in the middle of the night definitely fell into the category of things you didn't know were going to happen!

'Indeed you don't,' he agreed.

'And it would be awful to spend your last moments regretting all the things you *didn't* do.' She studied his face, trying to read his reaction. 'You do understand what I'm talking about?'

'So you've decided to do all those…*things*?'

She nodded.

'And you decided that now was as good a time as any to start?' he prompted thickly.

'I just thought maybe you…' I just thought the man who could have literally any woman he wanted would want me. 'No pressure, obviously,' she added gruffly. 'You're probably recalling that I said I wasn't very good at sex…'

There was a long pause and she thought in dismay, He's thinking of a way to let me down gently.

'No, that isn't what I'm thinking. No pressure…' He started across the room towards her. 'No pressure…?' he said again, before grabbing his head in both hands and groaning. 'You want to know what pressure is, *querida*?' He took her chin in one hand and tilted her head up to his.

A primal fire burnt in his blue eyes as they moved over her delicate features.

His eyes remained meshed with hers as with one hand in the small of her back and the other wrapped around her narrow ribcage he casually hauled her towards him, pulling her close until their bodies were sealed at hip level.

'This,' he slurred, 'is pressure.' Fleur moaned, her eyes

closing as she felt the throbbing imprint of his erection pulsing into the softness of her belly. 'That,' he rasped huskily, 'is what you do to me. That is the pressure I have been feeling since the first moment I set eyes on you.'

Fleur, her eyes locked onto the hypnotic glow in his, was finding it increasingly difficult to form words. 'And do you still want to do something about it?'

The glitter in his eyes made her dizzy; she tried to look away and couldn't. They drew her like a magnet...*he* drew her like a magnet.

'This,' he said, taking her face tenderly between his hands.

'This is good...' she whispered as he kissed the corner of her mouth, a light butterfly kiss that released a flood of liquid heat low in her belly.

Antonio tilted her head to one side and kissed the pulse spot at the base of her slender throat. She looked at him through heavy lids and Fleur's vision blurred as she heard him say, 'You are so beautiful. I have dreamt...'

Her limbs were heavy and she was floating. Her breathy gasp was barely audible. 'Dreamt about what?'

'About being inside you,' he explained, before inserting his tongue between her parted lips.

Fleur moaned into his mouth and kissed him back.

His hands moved down over her back to cup her bottom and pull her hard against the cradle of his narrow male hips, hard against the erection that ground into the softness of her belly.

'Make love to me, Antonio.' The sensual invitation in her golden eyes took his breath away.

'What have you got on under this?' he asked, sliding his hand down the neck of the big towelling robe she wore.

'Well, they gave me one of Tamara's nightdresses and it didn't seem...*appropriate* under the circumstances...' Said circumstances being that she was about to seduce the owner's father. 'So I took it off.'

'Which translates as nothing.' His smile smouldered.

'Uh-uh…what are you doing?'

'This,' he purred, giving the tie on her robe another sharp tug. She went automatically to catch hold of the fabric as it parted, but Antonio was faster.

He caught her wrists and, shaking his head, held them at her side.

Fleur stood, her breath coming in short, shallow gasps as though she had been running. Behind her breastbone her heart was banging so hard he had to hear it.

Not for a second since he had imprisoned her hands had his eyes left her face. His expression was taut, his dramatic blue eyes fierce yet tender as he released her wrists and slowly slid the heavy robe off her shoulders.

It fell to the floor and Fleur closed her eyes, suddenly over-whelmed by her insecurities.

She was standing there stark naked in front of possibly the most perfect male on the planet. She thought about how Adam's sly digs about her figure—she either had too much or too little, depending on which celebrity he was comparing her to—had hurt even though she had tried to forget the comments as well as the man.

The realisation that Antonio had been to bed with those perfect women made the memory of those scathing compar-isons even worse.

'Open your eyes.'

'Please stop looking at me. I…I'm…' She stood there, her eyes tight shut, her entire body racked by febrile shudders.

He took her face between his big hands. He was close enough for her to feel the warmth of his breath on her cheek as he rasped, 'Beautiful is the word you are searching for. My beautiful, bewitching little mermaid,' he purred. 'Open your eyes for me…' he coaxed.

She did and they immediately collided with his burning gaze.

'You are the most beautiful thing I have ever seen in my life.'

Words could lie but the eyes were the window to the soul and his were telling her everything she needed to know. His were telling her she was a desirable woman…hell, he should know! she thought, seeing herself through his eyes. It was about the most empowering feeling she had ever experienced.

'I have dreamt about this. I have dreamt,' he confided in a smoky voice that made her very conscious of the ache deep and low in her pelvis, 'of being inside you.'

Antonio's eyes were so dark they were almost black, she noticed as he slid one arm around her waist, the other behind her head, and said her name…his voice deep and not quite steady as he fitted his mouth to hers.

Then for some minutes she didn't think at all. The only things she was aware of were his mouth and tongue, his taste, and the searing heat of his hard, lean body burning into her as his skilful hands moulded her body to him.

She barely registered that he had lifted her feet clear of the floor until he lay her down on the big bed that was set centre stage in the room.

She lay there, one arm curved above her head, her hair tumbled around her passion-flushed face so beautifully wanton that his hands shook as he pulled at the cord of his robe. His eyes slid down the pale length of her exquisite body lingering on the apex of her thighs and the pink quivering peaks of her firm breasts.

His control slipped another notch as she smiled languidly and stretched out a hand to him.

'Come here.'

'*Por Dios!*' he groaned kicking aside the robe that had

fallen at his feet. 'You have no idea what just looking at you does to me.'

The smile that drove him slightly crazy lingered on Fleur's lips as her restless eyes slid down over the firm, powerful lines of his lean, rippling torso admiring the perfect marriage of grace and strength.

His broad shoulders and powerful chest. Then lower over his flat, taut belly ridged with perfectly defined muscles. Then lower still.

Her fractured gasp and wide-eyed, awed stare really tested Antonio's control to the limit.

He was breathing hard as he joined her. He kissed her mouth and felt the sigh shudder through her body as he ran his thumb across the engorged peak of her breast. Then he switched his attention to the other aching mound.

'You're so sensitive,' he said, raising himself up on one elbow to look down at her. He bent his head and flicked his tongue around the rosy areola.

'Oh, God!' Fleur gasped, looking down at the incredibly erotic image of his dark head against her breast.

Her fingers were tangled in his hair as he traced a line between the straining peaks and let his hand rest on the soft curve of her belly. He kissed her then, deep, drowning kisses, and all the while he stroked and touched her.

'I have to…I need…'

'What do you need?' he asked, sliding his hand down the silky inner aspect of her pale thighs. 'Do you need this, *querida*?'

A keening cry left Fleur as his fingers slid between her legs seeking the warmth and heat, the centre of her femininity and desire.

'Or this?' he asked, taking her hand and feeding it onto his own body.

His was velvet, hot and hard.

The sexual heat that flashed through her as she curved her fingers around him and felt him pulse against the pressure was white hot.

Her hand was trapped between their bodies as with a groan he rolled her onto her back.

He slid his hands under her bottom, lifting her hips as he knelt between her legs. Back arched, her head thrown back, Fleur looked at him through half-closed eyes.

'Please, Antonio…now I need…'

The fractured plea snapped his control. He could no longer resist the primitive urgency that pounded through his veins, and with one smooth thrust he entered her until he was totally sheathed in her tight, slick heat.

She let out a tiny cry.

Above her Antonio tensed, every muscle in his body screamed, but he held himself in check.

Fearing that he had hurt her, he said her name.

Her eyes snapped open.

She looked into his eyes; they were hot. She was hot; there was heat everywhere inside and out, fire in her blood; it was like drowning. The sensation of being filled, stretched by his velvet sheathed hardness was like nothing she had ever experienced or imagined.

'Don't stop.' Never, ever stop.

He responded in throaty, broken Spanish she didn't understand, but it didn't matter. This communication was not about words. And as he began to move, pushing into her, she tightened around him and pressed her fingers into the glistening firm skin of his golden sweat-slick back.

Fleur moaned into his mouth, arching her back to help him reach deeper inside her as the rhythm built…until it was not a separate thing. She was part of the rhythm and Antonio was part of her.

Then just when she thought it could not get any better her world exploded and she found it could.

Antonio felt her orgasm, felt the vibrations that rocked her, heard her hoarse, startled cry and watched her eyes fly open just moments before his own release.

He held her as their breathing slowed and their sweat-slick bodies cooled. Her head was on his chest.

She lifted her head and smiled at him. She looked glowing and luminous; she took his breath away. There was sleepy wonder in her face as she said, 'Well, that was a first.' His opinion of her ex-fiancé, never high, dropped even lower at this artless disclosure. 'Is it always like that for you?'

Antonio knew at that moment that he was in love.

Shaken by the discovery and also exhilarated, he stroked the hair from her cheek. 'No,' he admitted, 'but it will always be like that for us...or better.'

In the night he kept his promise, which Fleur had imagined was frankly impossible...twice.

CHAPTER THIRTEEN

'SEVEN weeks,' Huw said in a tone of mingled enquiry and wonder.

'I did not know you were counting.'

'Are you kidding? You're living with a woman. *You!*'

'Not according to Fleur. According to her we are sharing a bed.'

Huw studied the frustration and dissatisfaction on his friend's face and grinned. 'And is that different?'

'According to Fleur it is.'

'Keeping you at arm's length, is she?' Huw appeared to find the idea amusing. 'Well, what do you expect with a reputation like yours? She's a sensible girl.'

'I am so immensely grateful that you approve my choice of partner.'

Huw began to grin at the acid retort, and then stopped. 'Partner…partner as in bride?' He saw the expression on Antonio's face and sank weakly into a seat. 'Well, I'll be… When's the wedding?'

Antonio's expression was rueful as he recalled the conversation, which had taken place a week ago now. To prove he was still counting his friend had sent him a short and to the point email that very morning.

Eight weeks! When are you going to ask her?

It was a reasonable question. Fleur loved him; he knew she did. Was he stupid to wait to hear her say it?

The long-delayed trip home to Andalucia would be the perfect opportunity to claim his bride. His bride, the woman who had taught him to trust again, something he had not thought possible.

She had stood exactly here that very morning. He looked at the section of gravel in question and almost convinced himself that he could see the imprint of her feet.

Behind his half-closed eyelids Antonio could see her standing there, the light wind fluffing up her hair, blowing the thin robe she wore tight against her body so that he could see every soft, feminine curve. They had just made love, but looking at her had made him want to carry her back upstairs to their bed and start all over.

Instead he had kissed her.

His eyes darkened, the pupils expanding dramatically as he recalled the way she had wound her arms around his neck and twined her fingers into his hair, pressing her supple curves against him as she kissed him back with a passion, a desperation that had blown him away.

When she had pulled back there had been a look in her eyes—a deep sadness that had made him even more reluctant to leave her.

Antonio had been thinking about that look all morning; he had to know what it meant.

His feet made no sound as he walked into the bedroom. It was eleven a.m. and he should at this moment be taking an important, some might say vital, meeting.

Antonio would have agreed with them once, but the things that had been vital in his life two months ago had slipped down his order of priorities and others that he had previously lived in blissful ignorance of had risen to the top of the list.

Had it really been so blissful? Less complicated, sure…but would he really go back…to that place in his life where he had not been father to an awkward teenager?

Back to a time in his life when he had never heard of Fleur Stewart and she was not, albeit as she frequently reminded him *temporarily*, sharing his bed, and effectively his life.

A time when he would not have forgotten important papers, let alone come back for them personally. This morning it would have been an easy matter to send someone for them when he had realised the missing files were sitting on his desk at home.

His PA had been a little disgruntled when he had insisted on performing the task personally. Actually, a *lot* disgruntled. And he couldn't really blame her.

He felt a spasm of guilt when he recalled the horror on her face when she had caught up with him as he was about to leave. 'You do know how tight the schedule is today, don't you? And the Germans are due at…'

Antonio had turned a blind eye to her panic and told her warmly that he had every confidence in her ability to juggle things and keep everyone happy until he got back.

It was of course totally unprofessional and Antonio supposed he should feel some guilt, but he didn't.

He had a legitimate reason to see Fleur, or semi-legitimate at any rate, and he was going to take it. Nothing short of an act of God would stop him.

On one level he knew that his actions were totally illogical; he knew that putting at risk financial deals that had been months in the making for the sake of a brief glimpse of a woman he had kissed goodbye three hours earlier made no sense.

Even last week he might have tried to rationalise his actions, tell himself it was just sensational sex that drew him.

But he had moved beyond that. For several weeks his rigid emotional control had been slipping and today he had stopped trying to hold on to it.

Today he accepted the inescapable fact that she was in his blood, that he was totally addicted to everything about her, the entire package. The scent of her skin, her funny, lopsided smile and the fact she liked nothing better than to point out his faults. Well, no, he conceded, that wasn't totally true—she did like other things more.

There was a sensual glow in his eyes as his thoughts drifted back to her initial inability to believe that he could really get as much pleasure from satisfying her as he claimed. It was further evidence that the ex-boyfriend, who he already knew was an idiot because he had had the perfect woman and let her go, must have been a selfish and terminally unimaginative lover.

He had found that the simplest way to prove to her that he wasn't going to recoil in shock and horror if she told him what she enjoyed was to tell her what she did to him and what he wanted to do to her. It turned out several of their sexual fantasies dovetailed neatly.

Fleur was just removing a mobile phone from her ear when he walked up behind her. Curving one arm around her waist, he pulled her body into his. He slid his free hand under her jacket and caressed her breast through her blouse. As he kissed her ear lobe she released a long, sibilant sigh and relaxed back into him.

'I was thinking about you,' she whispered.

'You look very lovely,' he said, pressing kisses against the lovely line of her throat. 'Nice outfit—I'm going to enjoy taking it off…'

His seductive, smoky voice made her knees give. 'I've not

finished getting ready yet,' she protested, extending her bare foot to illustrate the fact.

Antonio slid a hand under the hem of her skirt and stroked the bare, silky curve of her smooth thigh. 'Do you have anything on under here?' he asked, moving higher.

'Yes, I do!' she squealed before moaning softly as his fingers tracked their way as far as the lacy edge of her pants.

'Pity, I was a little excited.'

'I can feel just how excited you are,' she retorted thickly. 'But it won't do you any good. I'm having lunch with Jane, remem—' She broke off and gasped as he turned her in his arms and kissed her lips, a long, lingering kiss that made her insides melt.

'Antonio,' she sighed when his mouth lifted. Dazed, her eyes lifted to his; the hot glitter in the dizzying depths of his blue eyes sent a rush of heat through her body. 'What are you doing here?' Not that I'm complaining. A slow, sensuous smile spread across her face as she extended her flexed fingers across his chest. Before laying her head against his heart.

'I forgot something,' he said, meshing his long brown fingers in the hair that lay loose on her shoulders. 'I'd say never cut your hair,' he admitted, pressing his lips to the crown of her shiny head and inhaling deeply the perfume of her shampoo, 'if I didn't think you'd react by going off and shaving the whole lot off. Should I try reverse psychology with you? Forbid you to touch my body—would you be all over me like a rash?'

Amazing how different Antonio's request was from her ex-fiancé's demanding attempts to control her. 'You could live with a trim, I take it?'

'You could be bald and I would still be your adoring slave.' I could live with anything so long as you were part of the package.

Her face still pressed to his chest, Fleur was oblivious to

the tension that drew the skin taut across Antonio's chiselled features. 'Did you say *you forgot…*?'

If living with him had taught her anything it was that Antonio never forgot anything. Her thoughts skidded to a halt. Even in the privacy of her own thoughts Fleur couldn't actually allow herself to say they were *living together.*

That this *wasn't* what they were doing was something she reminded herself of at least twenty times a day.

Living together was the next step along the commitment path when two people were in a relationship. It came before splitting up or marriage. What she had with Antonio was not a path to anywhere.

Antonio hadn't made any commitment. She was only here because of a freak set of circumstances. He had offered her a bed when she was homeless. It was temporary. When she was tempted to tell him how much she loved him, how her life would be empty without him, she said that one word to herself over and over…*temporary*!

It hurt but it worked.

The fact that they'd ended up sharing a bed for the past eight weeks didn't alter this situation. She was going to come out of this with a broken heart and nothing she did or said was going to change that. But if she didn't self-destruct and tell him how she felt she could still walk—or even stumble away—with her pride intact.

Pride and memories were better than nothing. You think, said the voice in her head.

Antonio flexed his shoulders, rotating his neck to release some of the knots of tension. 'I must be getting old.'

Fleur's head lifted. Her glance slid across the strong male contours of his bronzed vital features.

As she looked at him a wave of emotion welled up, building in intensity. Her inability to express the feelings that fought for release brought a light sheen of moisture to her smooth brow.

Control, she reminded herself. She needed to stay on top of her emotions, especially now.

Forcing a smile, she released a wry laugh. 'I think you've got a few good years yet.'

And even when he was old, she acknowledged, he would not lose the ability to turn female heads. It would take more than a few lines to dilute the raw sex appeal that was an integral part of Antonio.

What if he knew? Her jaw dropped a little as, rigid with horror, she loosened her grip on his shirt-front.

Antonio's hands fell away from her hips. His brows twitched into a frown as she stepped from his arms.

'Are you all right?' he asked, studying her porcelain pale face.

'Yes,' she said, forcing her lips into what she hoped was a perky smile. 'Why do you ask?' I'm being paranoid. There is *no* way he could know. She barely knew herself, and still didn't quite believe it.

'I don't know—you've seemed a little tense these last couple of days. What you need is a holiday.'

'Chance would be a fine thing.'

'Funny you should say that. I suggested to Tamara...' Antonio paused and Fleur, a puzzled frown on her face, waited for him to continue.

'I was expecting a ripple of applause or at least a word of praise,' he admitted, looking comically crestfallen.

'Why—what have you done?'

'I *suggested,* I did not command. I did not issue an edict or throw around ultimatums. You see what a moderating influence you are on me?'

Fleur, unable to resist his relentless charm, smiled back. 'Congratulations,' she said gravely.

'You see,' he said, running a finger down the curve of her cheek, 'how you are reforming me.'

'Once a wolf, always a wolf,' Fleur retorted. 'So what did you suggest?' she prompted.

'I suggested to Tamara that she might like to come home with me to Andalucia during part of her half-term break. Check out her new relations and the lay of the land…and so forth.'

'And she agreed?' Even a few weeks ago that would never have happened. But with each successive weekend that Tamara had come home from school Fleur had seen father and daughter become visibly more relaxed with each other.

He nodded.

'Oh, I'm so pleased for you, Antonio,' she said warmly. She knew how much this meant to him, how much he wanted the relationship with Tamara to develop and grow and how hard he had worked to make it happen.

Too hard sometimes.

When one day after a particularly loud row with Tamara he had asked her advice—at least, that was how Fleur had chosen to interpret his snarled, 'If you're so clever, what would you do?'—she had advised him to give the girl a little more space and stop trying to hothouse the relationship.

'It's a start, and you were right. It was better I did not push things too hard. One day she might even feel able to call me Dad.'

Fleur turned her head to hide the tears that sprang to her eyes. She doubted he was even aware of the note of yearning in his voice.

'So how do you feel about a week or two in Spain?'

Her face fell. *Me?*

'Who else would I be talking to? Yes, you—it is where I live.'

'I know.' And his heritage, Fleur realised, was apparent in the proud lines of his face and the vibrant warmth of his skin. The permanent groove above the bridge of his nose deepened as he studied her face. 'You don't look very pleased at the prospect. The college break does coincide with Tamara's half-term, doesn't it?'

'Yes.'

'Then you will come.' It was a statement and not a request.

'I'd love to, but I've made other arrangements.'

Antonio watched her eyes slide from his. With Fleur you didn't need a lie-detector test to know when she was lying. His jaw tightened. This was not going the way he had planned.

'What other arrangements?'

'Well, actually, no, I haven't actually made other arrangements,' she admitted. 'I actually—'

'You *actually* lied.'

Fleur heard the hard undercurrent of anger in his voice and grimaced. She lifted her eyes and read the hard suspicion in his. She had no control over the tell-tale colour that rushed to her face.

Biting down on her full lower lip, she stopped shifting her weight uncomfortably from foot to foot, aware that this did nothing to lessen her resemblance to someone who was as guilty as sin!

In reality the only thing she was guilty of was being in love with him.

'The idea of visiting my home and spending time with me is so abhorrent that you feel the need to lie.'

Fleur's eyes lifted. She stared at him, unable to believe he was serious. 'Don't be stupid! I spend every day with you.'

And nobody had even raised an eyebrow. She couldn't understand it. Was she the only one who seemed to find the situation in any way extraordinary?

Of course things might have been different if Tamara had, as she had initially predicted, reacted to the situation badly. But when Antonio's daughter, on her first weekend home from school, had caught them in a passionate embrace, the teenager had not only accepted, but displayed tacit approval of, the situation.

Antonio looked down at her. 'I am beginning to think that I have been stupid, very stupid.' For attributing her reluctance to admit her feelings as natural caution after a painful breakup. Concerned that he could frighten her off if he came on too strong, he had restrained himself with difficulty and not revealed his own feelings.

Maybe there were no emotions to be cautious about?

Had he been seeing what he wanted to see? It wouldn't be the first time. Only on this occasion he could not plead youthful ignorance.

'I didn't lie, exactly,' she protested, bewildered and confused by the depth of his sudden hostility. She could understand him being irritated because she hadn't fallen in with his plans, but surely the situation didn't warrant this sort of reaction.

He angled a sardonic brow. *'No?'*

'All right, then,' she acceded crossly. 'If you want to be pedantic, I lied, but not because…I just think that this trip should be about you and Tamara. How will she feel if you bring along your…?'

'Girlfriend? You are talking as though Tamara resents you. Nothing could be farther from the truth and you know it,' he accused.

'I'm not your girlfriend.'

'No? What are you, then? Mistress…lover…?'

'Oh, for heaven's sake!' she snapped. 'I don't know why you're being like this.'

'Mistress, lover, paramour, concubine?' he intoned cutting across her.

'This is a convenient arrangement, Antonio. You don't need to—'

'Convenient!' he thundered, throwing up his hands. His

voice was low and razor-edged as he observed, 'It is totally insupportable! My daughter calls me by my Christian name...'

'You told her to.'

Eyes narrowed, he dismissed her protest with a dismissive wave of his hand. 'And now the woman sharing my bed calls it a convenient arrangement...what should I read from this?'

Dismayed and a little confused by how swiftly things had deteriorated, she shook her head miserably, quashing the overwhelming urge to reassure him, to tell him the truth.

But she couldn't, not because she didn't know how he'd react. She knew *exactly* how he'd react, and therein lay the problem.

At that moment Fleur didn't think she'd have the moral fortitude to say no if he asked her to marry him. She would have even less moral fortitude in the romantic setting of his Spanish home! She had seen pictures. It made the Alhambra look like someone's backyard. The place looked like a film set specifically designed for the hero to propose to the heroine.

Her glance flickered downwards as her hand went to her stomach. Antonio had lost one child; he would never run the risk of losing another.

She knew that he would do anything it took to prevent that happening again. Even if that anything involved marrying a woman he didn't love.

She simply couldn't bear the idea of being the woman that came as part of the package.

'*Nothing...*' She ran the tip of her tongue nervously across her upper lip.

'Do you imagine I don't know there's something you're not telling me?'

Fleur could feel her fragile control slipping. 'For heaven's sake,' she accused, taking refuge in anger. 'You're twisting everything I say. And I've no idea why you're making such a big thing of it in the first place. I just don't think it's a good idea if I come to Spain with you. You need to spend quality time with Tamara.'

'I cannot spend quality time with Tamara when she is asleep.'

'So you're bringing me along to provide after-dark entertainment. Thanks very much—that makes me feel so special.'

'What other reason could I have for wanting to bring you along? For the pleasure of your charming company?' he suggested caustically.

'Well, as it will be dark, you won't mind it being someone else. I'm sure you won't have a problem filling the vacancy,' she observed bitterly.

'You think I wouldn't know you in the dark?' He took her chin in his hand and tilted her face up to him. 'And I don't want another woman in my bed. I want you.'

A deep sigh shuddered through Fleur's body as their eyes meshed. 'And I want to be there.'

He straightened up. 'Then it is settled. I will make the arrangements. We should be able to fly out Friday if I—'

She stared. 'I have just told you I am not coming.'

'You have also just told me, and, I have to tell you, you were *very* convincing, that you want to be in my bed.'

'Which doesn't mean that I'm going to do everything you say. I won't,' she told him, gritting her teeth, 'be manipulated or dictated to.'

His blue eyes narrowed. 'Why are you trying to pick a fight?' He broke off and cursed as the phone in his pocket began to ring. Still glaring at her, he flicked it open and held it to his ear. A few monosyllabic responses later he put it back in his pocket.

'I have to go.'

She gritted her teeth. 'Just when we were having so much fun.'

'We will continue this conversation later.'

'Always supposing I'm here,' she flung after his retreating back.

As the door closed she threw herself on the bed and punched the pillow in sheer frustration, then only moments later she leapt up and ran from the room.

By the time she reached the forecourt he was about to open the driver's door of his car. He saw her, but didn't stop.

Calling his name, she sprinted across the intervening yards oblivious to the gravel that dug into her bare feet. She was breathless and breathing hard as she reached him just as he slid into the seat.

'I will be here,' she said, urgency making her voice loud. 'I didn't mean it…' She stopped then, because she was crying big, gulping sobs that came without warning and convulsed her entire body.

Looking alarmed— As well he might, she thought, seeing as I'm acting like a mad woman—Antonio levered himself out of the car and took her by the shoulders.

And I can't even tell him it's just hormones, she thought, which made her cry even harder.

His hands slid down her arms, drawing her closer. '*Querida*…don't cry. I can take just about anything else. Scream, shout,' he suggested, tenderly wiping the moisture from her cheeks.

'S-sorry, I didn't sleep very well last night and—'

'Neither, if you recall, did I,' he reminded her as he picked her up as if she weighed nothing.

'It's really not—'

Antonio used the method he had perfected to make her shut up when she talked rubbish. He kissed her.

Placing her back on her feet in the hallway, he looked with concern into her pale face, noting the feverish ribbons of colour along her cheekbones.

Frustration was stamped on his face as he admitted, 'I really do have to go, but tonight,' he promised, tilting her face up to his, 'we will talk.'

As she watched him go the prospect of tonight filled her with dread.

CHAPTER FOURTEEN

'WE SHOULD do this more often. I really miss our chats,' Fleur said as she pushed aside her empty plate and smiled across the table at her best friend.

Jane raised a brow at the plate Fleur had set aside. 'I thought country air was supposed to give you a healthy appetite. You've just pushed that around your plate,' Jane accused, forking some tender lamb into her mouth.

Fleur shrugged. 'I'm not really hungry.'

Her best friend looked at her through the veil of her darkened lashes. 'Well, they do say that love can affect your appetite,' she observed slyly.

Fleur picked up her glass. 'Don't be stupid,' she said irritably. 'Do you think you bought everything you need?' She slanted a wry look towards the heap of bags on the chair beside Jane.

'You should have come along. That outfit you're wearing is so last season, darling. Trust me, I move in the most fashionable circles.'

Her exaggerated drawl made Fleur laugh.

'And I can still read you like a book,' Jane said in a quite different voice. 'You know, I've been trying to think of a word to describe the way you look, and I've just realised what it is…*haunted*.' She rested her chin on her steepled fingers and nodded. 'Yes you look haunted. So who's responsible for the Gothic under-eye shadows, Fleur?'

'You know, I don't think the holiday is such an incredible bargain if you take into account the small fortune you have spent on skiing gear.'

When Jane responded with, 'So you've moved in with him, then,' Fleur was forced to accept that her not-very-subtle attempt to divert the conversation into more comfortable channels had failed miserably.

'Moved in?' she echoed, playing for time.

'When do I get an invite? I can't wait to check out your Spanish stud. Is he as gorgeous in the flesh as he is in photos?'

Better; much, much better.

Fleur kept her expression carefully neutral as she denied Jane's labelling of the situation.

'Of course I haven't moved in. I've already told you it's a purely temporary arrangement while the builders are working on the cottage. I'm really very grateful, but he's not even there half the time.' And that half was pure agony.

'Eight weeks is not all that temporary,' Jane pointed out as she speared a baby onion.

'I have *not* moved in,' Fleur said, fighting to keep her cool in the face of her friend's unconcealed scepticism.

She still had a room. She just wasn't in it very often. What would be the point? Her toothbrush wasn't there, her belongings weren't there and, most importantly, Antonio wasn't there. It hadn't happened overnight. At first she had kept up the pretence and slipped to his room under cover of darkness.

Her insistence at keeping up appearances had at first amused Antonio, but he had grown impatient with her covert nocturnal creeping. Fleur didn't quite know how—the process had been insidious—but she and her toothbrush had ended up permanently based in his room.

'So you haven't moved in?' Jane mused, running a red fingernail around the rim of her wineglass.

'That's what I said.'

'So you're not living with him, you're just living in the same house and are sleeping with him and, please, *please*,' Jane begged, 'don't try and deny it. I can read you like a book,' she contended smugly as she watched the guilty colour fly to Fleur's cheeks. 'So what aren't you telling me…your best friend?'

Fleur gritted her teeth. 'There's nothing to tell,' she insisted.

'Living with one of the wealthiest and most eligible bachelors in Europe is some way off nothing!' The redhead exclaimed. 'I know I said you needed to get back out there, but I thought you'd start on the nursery slopes not go off-piste and jump off the side of a darned mountain first time out! *Antonio Rochas!* Fleur what were you thinking?'

Fleur's soft features tightened into a frustrated frown. '*Think…?*' she echoed. 'It's hard to think at all around Antonio. You have no idea what he does to—' She stopped as her powers of description failed her.

'I can imagine,' her friend retorted drily. 'You are aware that the man you are living with is notorious! He's a classic commitment phobe. He's broken more hearts than you and I have had hot dinners combined.'

'Will you lower your voice?' Fleur snapped, glancing nervously over her shoulder. 'And I've told you I'm not living with Antonio.'

'No, just sleeping with him.'

'Could you speak up, Jane? I think there's a couple of people at the next table who didn't hear you. Look, this is no big deal, it's casual, nothing more.' Fleur was congratulating herself on her amazing display of amused indifference when across the table her friend missed her mouth.

A look of almost comical horror spread across Jane's face. 'Oh, my God, you've fallen for him, haven't you?'

Fleur felt the colour rise up her neck, an incriminating stain. 'No...no, of course I haven't.'

Jane released a loud, fatalistic groan and covered her face with her hands. 'You have! Oh, Fleur!' she moaned reproachfully.

Fleur's chin came up defiantly. 'What if I have?' she demanded belligerently. 'I'm not saying I have,' she added in response to Jane's loud moan. 'But if I had it's not a crime.'

'It should be,' her friend rebutted with feeling. Her china-blue eyes were filled with genuine anxiety as she studied her friend's face. 'When are you going to learn to enjoy casual flings, Fleur?'

Fleur couldn't let this piece of blatant hypocrisy pass. 'Most people assume *you've* taken a vow of celibacy.'

'We're not talking about me. Why do you always have to fall in love?'

'I don't; I didn't love Adam—I was just too damn lazy. I couldn't act, I knew that I had to make a decision and I'm ashamed to admit he was the easy way out. I *wanted* to be in love, but I never loved him.'

'Well, that's something to be grateful for, two-timing scumbag that he was.'

'Antonio is different.'

'I wish for your sake he was, love, but—'

'Don't...just don't start bad-mouthing him, Jane. I know how he seems, but underneath he's actually quite a vulnerable person.'

Jane listened to this defence and gave a groan of horror. 'Oh, my God, Fleur, he's going to break your heart, you do know that, don't you?'

Of course she knew! Only she had been trying, and, up to this point, succeeding, in not thinking about it.

'I'll deal with that when it happens. Right now I'm going to enjoy today,' Fleur told her friend fiercely.

'And you can live with that?'

Fleur's slender shoulders lifted. 'I don't have any choice, Jane,' she admitted. 'Besides, I'm going to move out.'

'When?'

'Now.'

Jane stared as she got to her feet. 'What are you doing?'

'I'm doing the right thing for everyone. I'm moving out before he gets back. It's the only way,' she said half to herself.

'If he breaks your heart I'll kill him,' Jane hissed.

'I'd prefer you didn't kill the father of my child.'

Jane dropped her glass and sat there with red wine dripping on her white designer skirt. 'Oh, Fleur!' She gulped, her eyes going to Fleur's still-flat belly. 'Are you all right?'

Fleur nodded. 'More all right than I thought I would be,' she admitted. 'This baby is an accident, Jane, but I do want him.'

Tears started in the redhead's blue eyes. 'Have you told Antonio yet?'

Fleur shook her head. 'Not yet,' she admitted, her expression sober. 'Don't worry, I will, but I want to pick my time and place and I think it's best if I move back to the cottage first.'

'So you think he'll react badly? Men always blame the woman.'

'Oh, I'm not worried about that,' she admitted unhappily.

All men, Jane thought viciously, are bastards. Her expression compassionate, she got to her feet. Pulling a wad of cash from her wallet, she guided her friend between the tables.

'The thing I'm worried about,' Fleur admitted once they were outside, 'is that I'll say yes when he asks me to marry him. It might be easier not to in my own home, don't you think?'

'You think he'll propose when he knows about the baby?'

'I know he will. And I have to say no! Sorry,' she said, biting her lip. She gave a watery smile and blew her nose.

'I don't know what to say,' Jane admitted, handing her a fresh tissue.

'Well, that's a first.'

'Why?'

'Why am I so sure he'll ask me to marry him?'

'Well, I'd like to know that too, but I meant why would you be crazy enough to say no? I mean, we have just covered the fact that he is about the most eligible man on the planet. Sexy and rich—what more could a woman want?'

'I don't care about money or status.'

'Well, pardon me if I don't share your high-flying morals, but if Antonio Rochas asked me to marry him I don't think I'd hold the fact that he is loaded against him!'

'This isn't about money,' Fleur countered crossly. 'This is about avoiding a mistake I have already made, once before agreeing to marry a man who doesn't love me because I'm pregnant. And save all this hard-bitten cynical stuff for people who don't know you the way I do. You may have built yourself a hard shell, Jane, but deep down you're still the same old softy you always were. You would no more marry a man you didn't love than I would.'

'Humph,' Jane scoffed, '*I* believe that love is a chemical imbalance, a form of temporary insanity. And *I* believe that all men are genetically incapable of fidelity.'

Fleur caught her friend's hand and pressed it. 'I'm really sorry, Jane, that Luis—'

'*Don't* say that name,' Jane snapped urgently.

'Sorry.'

An uncharacteristic blush suffused her friend's cheeks before she recovered and inserted in a sarcastic drawl,

'Leaving my own disaster to one side, I'm assuming that you love this Rochas bloke…?'

Almost imperceptibly Fleur nodded her head. 'But he doesn't love me.'

'How can you be so sure?' Jane studied her friend's expression and sighed. 'You're not going to tell me why, are you?'

'No. I'm sorry, Jane, but—'

'Forget it. Oh, well,' she said, hailing a taxi, 'if you're going to be infuriatingly cryptic I'm not going to press you. But, whatever happens, for what it's worth I'll be here.'

CHAPTER FIFTEEN

THE wheels of the Jaguar sent up a shower of gravel as Antonio came to a screeching halt on the forecourt.

He slammed the door, but didn't immediately go inside. He didn't trust himself. He stood, hands clenched at his sides and breathing hard, as he fought to contain the fury that threatened to consume him.

She had stood there and said, 'I will be here.' And now she was leaving.

In the hallway, Tamara, who had obviously been waiting for him, jumped up from the bottom step.

She waved the phone that was clutched in her hand as greeting when she saw him. 'I thought you'd never get here!' she exclaimed when she saw him.

'Has she gone yet?' Not that it would make any difference; it didn't matter where she went—he would follow.

'No, not yet, but she will unless you do something. You really can't let her go. Fleur belongs here.'

Antonio, who was moving towards the stairs, flashed his daughter a taut smile. He couldn't have put it better himself. 'Don't worry, she won't be going anywhere,' he promised grimly.

'The phone—you have to take this call.' Tamara waved the receiver towards him. 'This woman, she won't go away. She's been hanging on for twenty minutes.'

Antonio was uninterested. Mentally he was already confronting Fleur. Explaining to her that their lives were inextricably linked, that there was a reason that they had met as they had. They were destined to be together. 'Hang up.'

'She says if I do she'll tell every newspaper in the country what a total—sorry, her words—*bastard* you are, and then she'll come here and—'

'The woman is insane,' he cut in impatiently.

'Yeah, I know, but this lunatic says she's Fleur's best friend.' Antonio stilled then, and held out his hand.

As her father took the receiver from her hand Tamara said softly in his ear, 'Keep Fleur with us, Dad. She belongs.'

As Antonio recovered from the shock of hearing himself addressed as *Dad* for the first time, a slow smile spread across his lean face and he lifted the receiver to his ear.

'Hello, Fleur's friend, this is Antonio Rochas. I can't talk now—I'm about to go propose to Fleur, the woman I love.' He heard a sharp intake of breath just before he handed the phone back to Tamara, who gave him a thumbs-up sign as he mounted the stairs.

Antonio stopped in the doorway and willed his mind to empty and his body to relax. The mental exercise normally required no conscious effort on his part; on this occasion finding his inner calm had never been more difficult.

Any calm he had achieved vanished the moment he walked into the room. Sexual hunger wiped everything else from his mind.

Wearing a pair of snug jeans and a tee shirt she was bent over the bed. In profile her expression was pensive, as he watched she lifted the weight of her hair off her neck and rolled her shoulders.

He weakly allowed himself to be distracted by the combination of her delicious behind and her neck. For a moment he actually forgot what he was here for as he played out a scenario in his head that involved throwing her on the bed and peeling off her clothes.

His fingers flexed as he imagined the fine muscles contracting under the satin-smooth surface of her skin as his fingertips traced a line between her heaving breasts, then teased each puckered, straining peak with his tongue and teeth until she cried out. Thinking about that choked little sound in the back of her throat made the insistent throbbing ache in his groin intensify.

Fleur was conscious of his silent presence before he spoke, but then she was so fine-tuned to Antonio that she wouldn't have had a problem locating him in a crowd of a thousand other golden-skinned, dark-haired, utterly perfect-looking men, always supposing the planet contained that number!

'What are you doing?'

God, but I love that voice. I love the person with the voice... The possibility that very shortly it would not be the first thing she heard when she awoke each morning filled her with a bleak despair.

It's just the way it is, the tough voice in her head told her—so get used to it!

That was never going to happen, but at least she could emerge from this with some dignity intact. Nobody automatically qualified for happiness, she reminded herself; others coped and so would she.

And I'll have his baby.

Fleur knew that short term it would have been much easier to marry him, but in the long run she knew that she was doing the right thing.

If she couldn't have his love, what was the point?

Her hands were shaking; had he noticed? Absurd question. Of *course* he'd noticed. Antonio noticed everything—a circumstance that made the fact he hadn't yet cottoned on to the fact she was out-of-her-mind, head-over-heels in love with him all the more astonishing.

'You haven't answered my question, *querida*.'

She turned her head then, the pallor of her skin accentuated by the thin ribbons of colour across her cheeks.

Just looking at him standing there looking impossibly gorgeous in a dark, fallen-angel way made her senses leap.

She ran her tongue across the dry outline of her lips and swallowed. 'I'm packing, Antonio.'

He folded his arms across his chest the gesture casual, but not his expression. She could almost feel the burning track of his shimmering eyes as they moved hungrily over her face.

As their glances locked the tension in the room was electric.

'And *why* are you packing, *querida*?'

Though not raised above conversational level, his soft-accented drawl hit her with the force of a sonic boom.

'The reason most people pack. I'm going back home, Antonio.' Only it didn't feel like home any more.

There was a pause. His voice was flat as he said, 'I would have come back and found you gone. You told me you would be here when I got back. I believed you.'

Fleur struggled to maintain her outer illusion of control even though she was leaking calm like a sieve.

'I changed my mind, as the work on the cottage is done and I got back earlier than I thought.'

'And you thought, What can I do? I know, I can run out on Antonio, because it will be such fun to think of him coming home and finding me gone.'

'Believe me, I'm not having fun.' She took a deep breath and fought to contain her feelings. After a short, painful silence during which her nails gouged deep half-moons in the soft flesh of her palms she managed to sound almost composed as she reminded him, 'This was only ever a temporary arrangement.'

Her bright smile was brittle as she added, 'My house is fixed.' Shame they couldn't fix broken hearts because hers felt as though it were on the point of shattering. 'The insurance company signed off the work at the weekend...I never intended to...'

'To what?'

To fall in love with you.

Her gold-flecked eyes slid from his as she began to tap her fingertips nervously against one another. 'To stay this long,' she substituted huskily. 'And we can still see one another...if you want to. I just need my own space.'

'No, you don't.'

It was a struggle to counter such rock-solid arrogance and certainty, but she tried to sound amused. 'How do you know what I need?' This was going even worse than her worse-possible-scenario version.

'You've told me often enough. What you need, Fleur, is me. Have you forgotten?' he taunted silkily. 'Shall I remind you?'

As if I need reminding. 'That's pretty arrogant even for you, Antonio. You can't take literally what someone says in...' Her eyelashes swept downwards. She didn't look up as he walked up to her, didn't react as he stopped so close that she could feel the heat radiating from his hard male body.

'In bed?' he suggested, his smoky voice laden with husky suggestion. 'We weren't always in bed.'

The reminder sent a series of images shocking in clarity dancing across her retina. Her nostrils flared, she could almost smell the musky scent of their lovemaking.

'My desire to make love to you has never been restricted to the bedroom or the hours of darkness.'

'I never said you lacked imagination sexually.'

'You'll never find what we have together with another man. You do know that.'

Of course she knew that!

With each sinfully seductive word the pressure in her head built up. And so too did the growing lassitude in her limbs. Trembling, she shook her head in mute denial.

'Could you bear never having me touch you again…like this?'

He reached out and ran his thumb down the soft curve of her cheek.

Pupils dilated, Fleur gazed helplessly into his dark face. 'I'll never stop wanting you.' The raw admission was torn from her throat.

Triumph, primitive and male, flared in his eyes.

'But this isn't about wanting. We can't always have what we want,' she told him sadly.

'That is a defeatist attitude.'

'I'm a realist.'

'I envy you. Me, I'm a hopeless romantic.'

Her golden eyes opened to their fullest extent. *'You!'*

'We all have secrets—now you know mine…or at least one of them. How about you return the compliment and tell me the real reason you are going?'

Hand pressed to her trembling mouth, she stepped backwards shaking her head. 'I'm not doing this. I can't. You can persuade me to do most things, but not this. I *have* to go.'

As panic seized her she shook her head to clear the sensual haze that clouded her senses. The back of her knees made contact with the foot of the bed, pretty fortuitous as Fleur wasn't sure how much longer her rubbery legs would hold her up. She sat down heavily on the silk cover.

'What are you doing here anyway?' She raised her

accusing eyes to his lean, saturnine face. 'You're meant to be in London until tonight.' If they were going to have this conversation at least then it would have been on her territory.

'By which time you wouldn't be here,' he said flatly. 'I'm sorry to spoil your plans, *querida*.'

The dark irony in his tone made her wince. 'You didn't say why you changed your mind.' She stopped and stared. Comprehension finally dawned and her eyes widened. 'Tamara rang you, didn't she? She said she wouldn't.'

Antonio didn't deny or confirm her accusation. 'You didn't have to go to such elaborate lengths to leave. I would have helped you pack if you'd asked me.'

His words hit Fleur like a knife sliding between her ribs. 'You *would*?' Was he bored with her already? Well, that made things simpler.

'Certainly,' he said smoothly. 'If you had first been able to tell me that you didn't enjoy sharing my bed. That you didn't love me?'

The remaining blood drained from Fleur's face. 'I have *never* said I loved you!' she protested tremulously.

The smugness she might have expected to hear was absent from his voice when he inserted throatily, 'No, but you have had to bite your tongue on occasions, haven't you, *querida*?'

Was I that obvious?

Fleur was mortified beyond belief, every inch of her skin burning; it was only the remnants of her pride that stopped her running from the room right then. But she knew that it would only be delaying the inevitable. This was one confrontation that she couldn't run away from any more than she could run away from her feelings for this man.

'As you know everything,' she said, refusing to play the truth-telling game, 'there isn't much point in prolonging this discussion, is there?'

'Maybe,' he responded in an odd, driven voice, 'I need to hear you say it.'

Fleur stared at him and thought, Why are you doing this to me? Was there some thread of cruelty in his nature that she had not seen until now?

'And I need,' she said briskly, 'to pack. You don't need to worry about giving me a lift. Jane is coming over to—'

'The same Jane who thinks I am a bastard?'

'What are you talking about?'

'She rang here.'

'She has my mobile number.'

'She rang me, not you. It seemed she had a lot to tell me.'

Fleur's brow puckered. 'What would Jane have to tell you?'

'Other than the fact I am a bastard, you mean? Actually I have—'

'Oh, my God!' Suddenly Fleur knew what he was going to say. The colour drained from her face, leaving it paper-pale.

Jane had blabbed! She couldn't seem to help herself when it came to interfering.

Had she stopped at telling Antonio about the baby, or had she not been happy until she'd revealed Fleur's true feelings for him?

Fleur felt her world tilt and she grabbed the first thing that came to hand, which happened to be her suitcase. The case and the contents went tumbling to the floor. Fleur dropped down to her knees and began to bundle up the spilled clothes haphazardly.

For this, she thought grimly, she would never, ever forgive Jane. She had well and truly stepped over the line this time.

Antonio, who had watched with alarm as she disintegrated before his eyes, caught her arm and hauled her to her feet. The clothes she held against her chest spilled to the floor as he spun her to face him. As she lifted her face to his he saw that her glorious eyes were brimming with unshed tears.

'So,' she said, expelling a fractured sigh, 'now you know about the baby.'

Antonio stiffened. There was a baby? His brain seemed to be working with tortuous slowness so it was several seconds before it produced a stunned. *My baby!*

'*Jane…*' Fleur said, her face tight with anger. 'Well, she had no right, no right whatever, to tell you. Why,' she wondered, voicing her resentment, 'does she always have to butt in?'

The Jane woman, Antonio realised, might not be quite the nightmare she had always sounded to him. '*Baby…?*' He swallowed and ran a hand across his jaw. 'You are pregnant.'

She saw the stunned, almost punch-drunk look on his face and covered her mouth with her hand. 'You didn't know, did you?' She shook her head in numb disbelief. 'Jane didn't say anything.'

Antonio's eyes were trained on her belly. 'She didn't get the chance. I hung up on her. You're carrying my baby. I suppose there is a perfectly good reason you didn't mention it in passing?'

'I was going to tell you. Antonio I know it looks…but, really, this is for the best.'

'And you decide what is best?'

'Please, Antonio.'

'Please, Antonio,' he mimicked. 'Please, Antonio, *what? Let you go…?*' He vented a laugh, but there was no laughter in the incandescent blue eyes that meshed with hers. He shook his head. 'It is not going to happen, Fleur. You are carrying my child.'

'I knew that you'd react this way,' she cried miserably. 'That's why I didn't want to be here when… It would have been so much easier if I was at home.' Actually she was beginning to recognise that the protection of being on home ground of having her own things around her had only ever existed in her head.

This was always going to be tough.

'Look, Antonio, I do understand how this looks.'

'You do know that you are not making any sense?'

Fleur sniffed loudly and yelled, 'Of *course* I know I'm not making any sense.'

His abrupt strained laugh took the edge off the explosive tension between them.

'I suggest that you sit down.' He studied her face and added drily, 'Before you fall down, and then you can start at the beginning and tell me what this is about. Are you angry with me because of the baby? I realise that having another child must bring back—'

'No…no,' she said quickly.

'We will do this thing together, Fleur. You will not be alone.'

He sounded so sincere and so caring that she had to gulp back a sob. 'I know I won't,' she said quietly. 'And there is no reason that this pregnancy should go wrong—at least, that's what the doctors told me.' Her light laugh could not disguise the fact that, despite medical advice, she was not going to relax until this baby was born safe and sound.

And I'll be there, Antonio thought. If he was going to be of any use to Fleur he needed to be clued up. He realised there was a lot he needed to learn, because when the time came he didn't want any doctors blinding him with science.

When he heard her admit, 'I was shocked when I realised how much I wanted *your* baby, not as replacement for the one I lost, just for him or her.' She responded to the pressure from the hand on her shoulder and sank back onto the bed.

She hadn't said 'my' baby or 'the' baby, she'd said 'your' baby. 'I want our baby too,' he replied.

'You don't have to say that, Antonio. In fact,' she admitted in a small voice, 'I'd prefer you didn't.' Fleur's head fell forward onto her chest, spilling pale hair across her face.

Antonio placed a finger under her chin and tilted her face up to his.

'Why am I not allowed to express my feelings?'

'They're not your feelings, not really,' she said sadly.

'Am I not a better judge of what my feelings are than you?' he demanded, regarding her with an expression of baffled frustration.

'You don't have to pretend.'

'*Dios!*' he groaned. 'Why can you not believe me?' There was white-hot seething frustration in the cerulean eyes, which fastened onto her tear-streaked face. 'I am serious enough to ask you to be my wife. This is not how I planned to propose, but…' About to drop down on one knee, he stopped as Fleur gave a gulping sob. 'What is wrong?'

'*Everything!*'

'Can you be a little more specific?'

Fleur gave a sniff and scrubbed her wet face. 'It's really nice of you to pretend that you were always going to propose. I do appreciate it, but if you propose to me I have to warn you there's every chance I might say yes.'

'And that is a bad thing?'

Her tragic tear-filled eyes connected with his. 'I couldn't be happy married to someone who doesn't love me.'

Antonio laughed. 'Is that all? Then let me—'

'No!' Fleur reached across and pressed a hand to his mouth. 'Don't say it!' she pleaded. 'I couldn't bear it. Do you think,' she asked him miserably, 'I don't know that under *normal* circumstances you'd never ask me to marry you?'

Antonio took her wrist and pulled her hand from his mouth, but did not release it. Instead he kept it pressed to his chest.

Fleur closed her eyes. She could feel the thud of his heartbeat vibrate through her fingertips. 'I knew this would happen.'

He let go of her hand. 'At least you know what's happening. That puts you way ahead of me.'

Her vision blurred by unshed tears, Fleur opened her eyes and watched him stalk to the other end of the room. At the far end of the room he turned on his heel and dragged an unsteady hand through his hair. 'Is the idea of being my wife so abhorrent?'

She gulped back a sob and angled a resentful glare at his face before taking a deep breath. 'You know it isn't. But I can't marry you just because I'm pregnant.'

Antonio clasped a hand to his forehead and released a frustrated groan. 'I don't believe this is happening!'

'I know, I don't know how it happened either.' Despite the strangled choking sound that issued from his direction Fleur's gaze remained fixed on the toe of her shoe as she plunged on.

'You were so careful. But it did, and there it is. Obviously with your history you'll…well, want to make this…well, erm…do the conventional thing—I expected that. But what you have to understand is this isn't the same as the last time.'

'No, it is not.'

Her eyes finally lifted. Apprehensively she studied his face, trying to gauge his reaction. He actually looked *almost* composed, if you discounted the febrile glitter in his eyes.

'Well, obviously, for starters there's no way this baby won't know you're her father. I want to make that quite clear.'

'And?' he prompted.

She took a deep breath; if ever a situation had called for a brave face, this was it. Despite her best efforts there was a telltale catch in Fleur's voice as she pointed out the obvious.

'Well, you're not in love with me the way you were with Tamara's mother.' And that made all the difference in the world. 'Do you think I don't know how you feel about missing out on her growing up? I catch you looking at her sometimes and I can see you…' She had to clear her throat before she could go on.

'Do you think I don't see that hurt and loss in your face every day? I know that you'd do anything for that not to happen again…even,' she said with a small, bleak smile, 'marry me.'

He started to walk towards her then, his tread slow and measured. If a walk could be explosive, his was. He was exuding raw, rampant masculinity from every gorgeous pore.

A whimper trapped in her throat, Fleur, her enthralled eyes wide, slithered backwards on the silk quilt tucking her feet under her and clasping her knees protectively.

He stopped about an inch from the foot of the bed.

'*Por Dios*. What makes you think I was in love with Miranda?'

'I'm not stupid, Antonio.' Though falling in love with a man who didn't and couldn't love you back hardly made her the sharpest knife in the box.

One dark brow lifted. 'I think you might like to explain that one to me.'

Her gaze drifted away from his. 'I heard Tamara ask you that night in the hospital,' she confessed huskily. 'And I heard you say—'

'I know what I said,' he cut in. 'Think about it, Fleur,' he suggested.

It was on the tip of Fleur's tongue to inform him that she had spent too much time already dwelling on that particular theme when she realised the confession would relieve her of what little dignity she still retained!

'What else would I say to my daughter? That her mother was a cold, manipulative, avaricious bitch?'

Fleur's face went blank with shock. 'What are you talking about?'

'I'm talking about the fact that Miranda was a sexual

predator without a single moral scruple to her name,' he explained contemptuously.

'But you loved her!' Fleur protested.

And didn't they say love and hate were closely related? When relationships went sour, bitterness built up. Was that what had happened? Had Miranda rejected him? The idea of any woman rejecting Antonio seemed pretty far-fetched to Fleur, but...

Suddenly she couldn't speculate any more. She lifted a hand to her spinning head; she didn't know what to think.

In a state of total confusion, she heard his voice through the distant dull roar in her ears.

'I imagined I was in love with her, yes, I did, but I was nineteen. Boys of nineteen are not renowned for their discrimination when it comes to women.'

Fleur's hand dropped from her face. *'Nineteen?'*

His brows lifted as he directed a sardonic look at her shocked face. 'And here was I thinking I looked a fairly well-preserved thirty-three. I would have thought you would have worked out the maths by now, *querida*,' he teased softly.

'I know you were young. It just didn't hit home how young until now. Was there opposition from her family?'

'Opposition...?' There was a furrow between his brows as his piercing blue gaze moved across her face. *'Madre mia,* the way your mind works is a constant source of amazement to me,' he revealed. 'You are you imagining some star-crossed lovers' scenario, aren't you? Nothing,' he revealed with a hard laugh, 'could be further from the truth. Miranda Stiller was a woman of thirty when we met. She didn't need parental consent for her actions. I seriously doubt if she ever had.'

'Thirty...' Fleur echoed, her face going blank with shock. 'But I assumed that...'

He lowered himself onto the edge of the bed and took her

chin in his hand. With deliberation he captured her restless gaze with his own, and held it. 'You assume a great deal. Your assumptions are rarely correct.'

'You have to assume when someone doesn't volunteer any information.'

'Not volunteer… You have no idea, do you?' When she looked at him in blank incomprehension, he shook his head.

'No idea about what?'

'No idea that I look at you and experience this strange urge to strip my soul bare.' The hard, driven quality in his voice was mirrored in his face. 'I have revealed more of myself to you in the space of a few months than any woman…*ever*. Now,' he added before she could respond to this amazing contention, 'let me reveal some more.'

'But—'

'No buts. Fourteen years ago I was spending my college break working at one of our hotels as a waiter.'

'Waiter!' she exclaimed, trying and failing utterly to mentally visualise Antonio in that role.

'In my father's day the company was exclusively involved in the hotel business. My father believed that to understand the business you needed to understand it inside out. He also thought that carrying bags and waiting tables would…erm… trim my youthful arrogance down to size.'

'It didn't work, then,' she said faintly.

His lips quivered faintly in response to her half-hearted jibe. 'Tamara's mother was a guest at the hotel where I was working. Miranda was beautiful…very beautiful.'

And he had been comparing every woman with this paragon since. Jealousy slid like a dull blade through Fleur's body.

'She was totally unlike the girls I knew. She seemed the epitome of glamour to me.'

The admission confirmed Fleur's worst fears.

Antonio's sensual mouth twitched into a self-derisory grimace as he added, 'You have to remember that I was nineteen and I'd not come across many high-class call girls at the time.'

'Call girl!'

'In all but name,' he said contemptuously. 'She may not have asked for money, but she used her body to get what she wanted. She had ambition and brains. Men were nothing more than stepping-stones for her, but I was for fun, not profit. Of course, if she had known that I stood to inherit a fortune the outcome might have been different, and when she rejected me my pride stopped me revealing my identity.

'She invited me to her room the first night. She seduced me—not that I am suggesting I was a total innocent or that I wasn't *very* willing to be seduced. For most teenage boys the older experienced woman is a fantasy.'

Fleur closed her eyes and shook her head. 'I really don't need to know the details. I'm sure there were reasons why you didn't stay together.'

Antonio leaned forward and, taking her chin in his hand, he tilted her face up to his. 'Where on earth did you get the idea that we were ever *together?*'

Fleur blinked as the tears started to spill from her eyes. 'Please, Antonio…'

He fitted his lips to hers and kissed her. If it had been intended to subdue or dominate she might have been able to resist, but the exquisite tenderness in the long, lingering kiss was something that was literally irresistible.

When his lips lifted from hers he did not pull away, but stayed there so close their warm breaths mingled intimately. He ran a finger down the curve of her cheek and nudged his nose against hers.

'Now you will listen, *querida*. No, please don't say any-thing,' he warned, placing a finger against her lips.

'I had an affair with Miranda. I did not completely lie to Tamara. I did think I was in love with her mother. Of *course* I thought I was in love! I was nineteen, I had a body bursting with hormones and, although you might find it difficult to believe, an incurably romantic nature.

'I don't deny that the experience left its mark on me,' he observed thoughtfully. 'I have become increasingly cynical and emotionally detached over the years. Not in response to any serious damage inflicted on my heart,' he added, pressing her hand to the area on his chest where that organ beat strongly, 'but rather to my pride. A woman made a fool of me so I determined that no other woman would ever have the op-portunity.

'I had no problem keeping women at arm's length. As my sister, a woman I feel you will have a lot in common with, recently observed, my relationships are actually one-night stands that last a little longer.'

A smile glimmered in the glorious depths of his eyes as he looked at her. 'Then I met you, my reluctant lover. And you were in my head from the first moment I saw you, *and*,' he added, his fingers tightening around the hand he held pressed to his chest, 'my heart.'

For Fleur it felt like the emotional equivalent of the sun suddenly coming out from behind a cloud after two months of gloom, even though her personal gloom had been inter-spersed by the odd inspired flashes of lightning.

Her eyes went from his fingers curled around hers to his face and a deep sigh shuddered through her body. She didn't dare believe what she was thinking; it was just too…too…*fantastic*.

'But I thought…' Her throat closed over as she read the message in his shimmering blue eyes.

'Do me a favour—do not think,' he begged.

The beginning of a tremulous smile formed on her lips. 'Am I allowed,' she asked, a quiver in her voice, 'to tell you something I *know*.'

His expression was grave and laced with caution as he nodded his assent to this suggestion.

'I know,' she said simply, 'that I love you, Antonio. I love you so much that the idea of not being with you makes me feel…*hollow*.' Her chin dropped to her chest. 'I don't suppose I'm making any more sense than usual,' she muttered.

'On the contrary, you are making total sense, but then this is a feeling I have also. I love you, Fleur Stewart. I think I did from the moment I saw you in that wood. It was my in- tention to ask you to be my wife when you came with me to Spain, so you see that is why I reacted as I did when you refused.'

Her face scrunched in a mask of incomprehension. This was an awful lot for someone who a few minutes ago had been looking forward to a lonely existence to take in.

'But you didn't know about the baby then,' she protested weakly.

With a sigh of exasperation he laid the heel of one hand in the centre of her chest and pushed. Fleur fell back against the bed and lay there as he lay down beside her, his weight sus- pended on one elbow.

'Are you not hearing what I'm saying?'

'Yes, but…'

Her lovely luminous eyes started to fill again and Antonio judged this was the moment to take charge. 'No buts. We have agreed I love you, *mi querida*, and you love me.'

'Oh, I do, Antonio,' she told him, her heart in her blissful smile. 'So much it hurts.'

'And I seriously doubt my ability to function unless I wake

up and feel you next to me every single day. And while I love the idea of us having a baby, I didn't even know about him until a few minutes ago.'

Finally she allowed herself to feel the rapture that she had been holding in check. 'Oh, Antonio, it felt like the past all over again. I didn't want you to be trapped into a loveless marriage where you'd end up hating me.'

'Hate you, *mi esposa*?' He shook his head in gentle reproach, frowning to see the pain on her face. 'It is not possible even when I want to put my hands around your neck and…' He was in the process of demonstrating this when a distracted expression drifted across his face. 'Such a lovely neck,' he breathed, then expelling a deep sigh, he lifted his eyes to her face and explained. 'Even when you drove me insane I still loved you more than my life.'

To hear this man whom she adored declare his love with such passionate simplicity was so moving that for a moment Fleur couldn't speak at all. When she did her voice shook with the depth of the emotion she felt.

'I can't believe you really want me…really love me?' she admitted, still blown away by the sheer wonder of it.

'Then you must,' he said, slipping the top button on her shirt, 'allow me to prove it to you.'

A smile spread across her face. 'You've got plenty of time to do that…just about the rest of our lives.' And Fleur for one had every intention of enjoying every precious moment.

'True, *querida,* but just now my need is…somewhat urgent.'

She responded to the throaty admission with a sultry smile that tore a ragged groan from his throat. 'You are killing me!' he protested.

'Is it possible to kill someone with love?' she asked innocently.

A white grin split his dark, lean features as he shook his

head. 'I have not the faintest idea,' he admitted, 'but I am willing to find out. If you will supply the love.'

Fleur sighed happily. 'For ever and ever,' she promised huskily. This was a promise she knew she would have no problem keeping.

REQUEST YOUR FREE BOOKS!

 HARLEQUIN *Presents* ®

PASSION GUARANTEED SEDUCTION

2 FREE NOVELS PLUS 2
FREE GIFTS!

HP07

I ❤ HARLEQUIN® *Presents*

BROUGHT TO YOU BY FANS OF HARLEQUIN PRESENTS.

We are its editors and authors and biggest fans—and we'd love to hear from YOU!

Subscribe today to our online blog at
www.iheartpresents.com